R.L. STINE

GHOSTS OF
FEAR STREET®

HOW TO BE
A VAMPIRE

ALADDIN
NEW YORK LONDON TORONTO SYDNEY

ALADDIN
An imprint of Simon & Schuster Children's Publishing Division
1230 Avenue of the Americas, New York, NY 10020
This Aladdin paperback edition August 2011
Copyright © 1996 by Parachute Press, Inc.
How to Be a Vampire written by Katy Hall
All rights reserved, including the right of reproduction
in whole or in part in any form.
ALADDIN is a trademark of Simon & Schuster, Inc., and related
logo is a registered trademark of Simon & Schuster, Inc.
FEAR STREET is a registered trademark of Parachute Press, Inc.
For information about special discounts for bulk purchases,
please contact Simon & Schuster Special Sales at 1-866-506-1949
or business@simonandschuster.com.
The Simon & Schuster Speakers Bureau can bring authors to
your live event. For more information or to book an event contact
the Simon & Schuster Speakers Bureau at 1-866-248-3049 or
visit our website at www.simonspeakers.com.
Manufactured in the United States of America 0711 OFF
2 4 6 8 10 9 7 5 3 1
Library of Congress Control Number 2011920437
ISBN 978-1-4424-2760-0

1

"Let's move it, Andrew," Emily said to her brother. "I have tons of homework."

"Wait," Andrew whispered. "Just a second." He glanced around Shadyside Park. It was almost dark. They needed to stay only a few more minutes. Only until it was really dark. That's when they all came out. Everyone knew that.

Emily brushed a strand of her wavy red hair off her face. "Not just a second," she insisted. "Now."

Andrew couldn't stand it when Emily got bossy. She was only twelve and a half. Just a year older than he was. So what if she was a head taller? Did that give her the right to be Emily Griffin, Know-It-All?

1

Here's what really killed Andrew: Emily thought she was perfect! She thought she was so good at softball. So smart. She thought she had a million friends. Plus she always bragged about her great taste in clothes. Personally, Andrew thought she looked like a moron, running around school in her little pleated skirts and stupid fake pearls. But here was the biggest joke of all—Emily thought she was gorgeous!

Andrew knew he wasn't great looking. He was skinny. His hair was somewhere between brown and red. His eyes were plain old brown. He had a million freckles. But so what? Big deal. At least his nose wasn't stuck up in the air like Emily's.

"I must be losing it," Emily was muttering. "Why did I let you talk me into getting off the bus at the high school? It's a fifteen-minute walk home, at least. If I'd stayed on the bus, I'd be in my room now—halfway finished with my homework."

"Shhh!" Andrew said. How could he hear anything coming with her jabbering like that?

"Let's go!" Emily insisted. "Move it, Android."

Andrew made a face. Emily thought she was so clever when she called him "Android." But he had to let it go now. Keep his mind on other things. Important things. He started walking. His feet crunched the leaves on the path around the pond.

"Right now is when they wake up," he told his sister.

Emily frowned. "Who's *they?*" she asked.

"The creatures of the night," Andrew answered. He tried to sound mysterious. Maybe that would make her stop.

"What are you talking about?" She kept walking. "Owls?"

"Not owls," Andrew replied. "The undead. *Vampires.* See, the second day turns into night, they . . ."

"Andrew!" Emily shouted. "Stop! I don't want to know what's inside that diseased brain of yours."

"But it's true," Andrew insisted.

"Nothing about vampires is true!" Emily scoffed. "They don't exist!" She shook her head. "I keep telling you—you're getting a little old for make-believe monsters."

"Vampires aren't make-believe," Andrew said. "Real vampires have bitten real people in the neck. Really." He fished a book out of the pocket of his jacket. "It says so right here."

Emily snatched the book and read the title. *"Vampire Secrets."* She groaned loudly. "I can't believe I'm related to someone who reads this garbage!"

"It's not garbage!" Andrew protested.

"It is too," Emily said. *"I* read good books. I've read almost every book on Ms. Parma's literature list in the library."

Emily was always bragging about the big-deal books she read. Okay, they had big words. Andrew had to admit that. And they were as thick as dictionaries. But that didn't make them good. That only made her backpack about ten pounds heavier than his.

"I don't remember seeing *Vampire Secrets* on Ms. Parma's list," Emily went on. "Or that thing you were reading last week."

"You mean *The Mummies Are Coming?*" Andrew asked. "That was totally awesome."

Emily tossed *Vampire Secrets* back to Andrew. "Where do you get this trash anyway?"

"T.J. lent me this one," Andrew told her.

"Why am I not surprised?" Emily rolled her eyes. "T.J. is the only person in the world who's weirder than you are."

"He is not!" Andrew protested.

Emily laughed. "Okay. Maybe you two are tied for weirdness. All you and T.J. ever talk about is monsters. No wonder neither of you has any other friends." She began walking more quickly.

Andrew trudged along behind her. So what if he and T.J. loved talking about monsters? And reading monster stories? They were good. Really good. Emily didn't know what she was missing.

"Walk faster, Andrew," Emily commanded.

But Andrew kept stalling. He dragged his feet. If he took long enough, they might see a vampire. He thought they would.

Emily was heading for Division Street—and she was heading there fast. They'd never see a vampire on

Division Street. The streetlights were too bright there. Way too bright for a creature of the night.

"Wait, Emily. I, uh, twisted my foot." Andrew leaned against a big oak tree, gripping his ankle. Then he let out a small cry of pain, hoping Emily would be totally convinced.

"I'm not falling for that twisted-ankle story again." Emily marched on. "You tried that one on me last week. Remember?"

Andrew sighed. He took a few steps. Then stopped.

Something dark and shadowy was creeping up behind Emily. Andrew watched as it dodged from tree to tree.

"Emily, stop!" he called in a hoarse whisper. "Something's following you!"

Emily whirled around. "I'm not falling for any more of your stupid tricks, Andrew!" she warned him.

Andrew scanned the trees—and saw the figure.

A figure in a long, sweeping cape.

The dark form slid out from behind a giant oak, inching closer and closer.

"There he is!" Andrew shouted. "Behind you!"

"Yeah, right." Emily stood in place with her hands on her hips.

The figure stepped silently up to Emily.

It hovered over her.

"Emily, I'm not kidding." Andrew's voice quivered. "Run!"

Emily shook her head in disgust.

The figure raised his dark hands.

"Emily! Run!" Andrew pleaded.

Too late.

Andrew watched in horror—as a pair of twisted fingers lunged for Emily's neck.

2

Emily screamed.

Her cries pierced the chill November air.

She twisted in the dark figure's grasp, struggling to free herself. "A vampire!" she cried. "Help me, Andrew!"

Andrew didn't move. He stared at the caped figure. At his long fangs dripping with saliva.

"Andrew, do something!" Emily shrieked.

"Vat a screamer you are," said the creature of the night. He released Emily from his grasp. He spat—and his fangs flew into his black-gloved hand.

Andrew fell to his knees—and laughed.

"Oh, man!" he cried. "That was awesome, T.J.!"

Emily smoothed her hair. She centered her pearl necklace.

"You immature creeps," she growled. "You are so pitiful. You act like two-year-olds!" With that she whirled away from them. She marched toward the park exit.

"Oh, man!" Andrew said again. He watched his sister stomp angrily past the baseball diamond. "I wish I had that on video."

"You'd think she'd be used to it by now," T.J. said, shaking his head. "But she falls for our pranks every time."

T.J. picked up his backpack from behind a tree. He untied his cape and took it off. He folded it carefully and tucked it into the backpack. He placed his plastic fangs in their spot in his pen-holder compartment.

Andrew admired T.J. When he pulled a prank, he went all the way. T.J. wasn't very tall. In fact, he was short and stocky. But he'd slicked back his hair with some of his older brother's mousse, and somehow managed to look like a full-sized vampire.

Andrew admired T.J. for another reason. He was loyal to vampires. Andrew loved all kinds of monsters. Werewolves. Mummies. Ghouls. Swamp things. But T.J. stuck to vampires. He knew everything about them. He was a specialist.

"This was better than when we scared Emily with the King Kong mask," T.J. said. "It was even better than the time we slimed her."

8

Andrew grinned, remembering. He'd gotten in trouble for that one. Mega-trouble. But it was worth it. And Emily deserved it. She kept making fun of one of his monster books, *Alien Slime from Mars.* Then one night he and T.J. arranged for her to see some slime for herself. Andrew giggled, thinking about how she stared in horror as green goo dripped down from her light fixture. How it plopped right down on her head. He was pretty sure that, for a second, Emily believed it was alien slime from Mars.

The next morning, Andrew jolted awake. Somebody was screaming! Screaming his name! He sat straight up in bed.

"Huh?" he cried.

"Get up!" Emily shouted from the doorway of his room. "Now!"

With a groan, Andrew fell back onto his bed. He burrowed deeper under his covers. He shut his eyes. Clearly Emily had not forgiven him for the vampire prank.

"Turn off your stupid alarm!" Emily shouted.

Alarm? Oh. That's what was going *beep, beep, beep.* Andrew had been dreaming that a vampire was knocking on his window. The vampire said *beep, beep, beep.* Finally, Andrew got up and opened the window for him. What a stupid dream. A *beeping* vampire.

Still half asleep, Andrew reached a hand out from

9

under his blanket. He waved it in the direction of his clock. At last he made contact. He hit the alarm button. The beeping stopped.

"We are going to catch the first bus this morning, Andrew," Emily announced. "If you aren't downstairs in fifteen minutes, I'm leaving without you. I don't care what Mom says."

Andrew heard his sister stomp down the stairs. If Emily left by herself, their mom would have a fit. Shadyside Middle School was pretty far away from their development—but very close to Fear Street. Close to the Fear Street Cemetery. Scary things happened there. All the time. If you believed the stories . . .

Andrew believed them. He knew that on Halloween, ghost kids rose from their graves. They tried to get real live kids to play a game with them. The game was called Hide and Shriek. The object of the game was to take the live kids back to the grave!

And then there was Miss Gaunt. She used to be a substitute teacher at Shadyside Middle School. Before she died, that is. Now she haunted the cemetery. She was always out searching for new students to teach—forever!

Andrew's mother always told him that they were only stories—that she didn't believe there was any truth in them. But still, she liked Andrew and Emily to travel to and from school together.

With a groan, Andrew made himself open his eyes.

He needed more sleep. Much more sleep. He wished he hadn't stayed up so late the night before, reading. He wished he could sink back onto his soft pillow again. And close his eyes . . .

He jerked his head up. Any minute now, Emily would be back, screaming at him. He pushed himself up on one arm. Ow! His elbow hit the corner of his book. The one he'd been up reading half the night. *Running with Werewolves*. Boy, what a great story!

Now Andrew felt wide awake. He remembered where he left off in the story. Jason, the hero of *Running with Werewolves*, was about to join a werewolf pack.

Andrew had read all but the last few pages. He'd die if he didn't find out what happened. He glanced at his clock. He could skip brushing his teeth for once. And washing his face.

Andrew sat on his bed. His eyes skimmed the words. Jason was in big trouble. He was a werewolf now. But the head werewolf didn't want him in the pack. Jason and the head werewolf were about to engage in mortal combat! Only a werewolf can kill another werewolf. So one of them had to kill the other. Jason didn't stand much of a chance.

Andrew's heart pounded as the snarling head werewolf reached out his huge, hairy paws. Reached out and grabbed Jason's neck. He squeezed, tighter and tighter. Choking Jason.

11

Andrew lifted his eyes from the book to catch his breath—and a hand from behind clutched his neck!

Andrew tried to scream. But no sound came out.

A voice came from behind Andrew. "Be ready in ten minutes!"

It was Emily's voice.

Emily let go of Andrew's neck. Then she reached around and snatched his book.

"Hey!" Andrew cried. He leapt up. But he was too late.

Emily was running out of his room with the book.

Andrew chased her. "Give it back!" he cried.

Emily whizzed down the stairs. She stood at the bottom, shaking her head. "Be down here in ten minutes, Andrew," she said. "Or this book is history!"

Andrew sighed. He knew when he was beaten. He plodded back to his room. There, he pulled on a polo shirt and a pair of jeans. Maybe Ms. Parma had a copy of *Running with Werewolves* in the school library. But probably not. Andrew would have to wait to find out what happened to Jason. He'd have to ask Emily for his book back. She might make him get down on his knees and beg!

Andrew got dressed. All but his sneakers. He felt around under his bed. He thought his sneakers were under there.

His fingers hit something. Something cold as ice. Not a sneaker. Definitely not. Andrew grasped the cold thing. He dragged it out from under his bed—and found himself gazing at a book.

An old black book. It looked important somehow. Boy, did it ever feel cold. So cold, it stung his fingers.

The book had no title. Andrew ran his hand over the smooth black leather. *Why does this book feel like a frozen TV dinner?* he wondered. *And how did it get under my bed?*

He opened the book. A blank page stared back at him. Andrew flipped page after page. Blank, blank, blank.

"Andrew?" Mrs. Griffin called from the bottom of the stairs. "What's keeping you, honey? Emily's waiting!"

"Coming!" Andrew called back.

He tossed the book down on his bed. He rummaged around, found his sneakers, and stuffed his feet into them. Maybe he'd take the black book to school with him. Show it to T.J.

But—wait. That's who must have put the book under his bed—T.J.! It had to be T.J. It was definitely a T.J. kind of joke.

Andrew slipped his homework papers into his binder. He shoved his binder into his backpack. He reached for the black book. Then he stopped.

He squinted down at the cover.

It had been blank before. Totally blank. He was sure of it. But now spidery letters were beginning to appear. Old-fashioned letters—writing themselves onto the book!

Andrew could only stare and wait as the writing continued.

And then it stopped.

The title was complete.

Andrew felt his blood run cold as he whispered the words on the front of the book:

HOW TO BE A VAMPIRE

3

Whoa! What a cool effect! Andrew opened the book. Maybe T.J. had stuck a computer chip inside the cover. Or maybe the writing was some kind of high-tech invisible ink. He couldn't tell. But . . . hey! Now writing began to appear on the first page! The words shimmered into view:

CHAPTER 1

VAMPIRES-IN-TRAINING

How did T.J. do these amazing effects? Brrr. And how did he make it so cold? Had T.J. surrounded it with cold packs from his freezer? How else could it stay so icy?

Andrew turned another page. More writing began to appear.

How would you like to sleep all day? Then, at sunset, turn into a wolf. Or a rat. Or a red mist. Or maybe a bat.

How would you like to fly? To pass through a closed door? Or a thick stone wall? Does all this sound too good to be true? It isn't. All you have to do is become a vampire.

How can you do this? One way is to be bitten by a vampire. The most popular place for this bite is on your neck. Once you are bitten, you are a vampire-in-training.

"Oh, wow," Andrew whispered. This was even better than *Running with Werewolves!* How did T.J. manage this stuff?

If it was T.J.

And . . . if it wasn't? Andrew swallowed. He didn't want to think about that. Because if T.J. didn't hide the book in his room, then . . . who did? Not Emily. She'd never think of anything like this. Not his mom. It had to be T.J.

"Andrew?" His mother's voice came from down the hallway.

Quickly, Andrew shoved the black book under his pillow. He fell to his knees. He pretended to be looking for something under his bed. He didn't want his mom to see what he'd been reading. He didn't want to answer any questions about the black book.

"Honey?" His mom stood in the doorway.

"Oh, Mom! Hi!" Andrew said. He kept searching. He realized something. There weren't any cold packs under his bed.

"Emily is having a fit because you're taking so long," Mrs. Griffin said. "Is anything wrong?"

"No!" Andrew's voice hit a high note. "Nothing's wrong! I can't find my sneakers. That's all."

Mrs. Griffin glanced at Andrew's feet. "You're wearing them, dear," she pointed out.

"Oh, right," Andrew said. He pulled his head out from under his bed. "I mean, I couldn't find them. And then I found them. Under my bed. There they were. So . . . I better tie them."

Andrew always babbled when he didn't know what else to do. Now he bent down and began tying his laces. Then he stood up.

"Are you sure you're okay?" His mother brushed his hair off his face. She put a hand to his forehead. "Hmmm. No temperature. But you are a bit clammy." She stepped back. "And so pale," she added. "I think you may be coming down with something."

"I feel fine," Andrew said. "Really."

No way could Andrew stay home. Not today. He

had to go to school. He had to find out what the story was with this book.

"Tell Emily we'll make the late bus," he said. He brushed by his mother on his way down the hall to the bathroom. "Tell her I'll be down in three minutes," he called.

"I'll butter a bagel for you," Mrs. Griffin called back to him. "You can eat it on the bus."

Andrew locked the bathroom door behind him. It was a habit. A lifelong habit of keeping out Emily. Of protecting his privacy. As he reached for his toothbrush, he heard footsteps in the hallway outside the bathroom. He smiled.

"Speed it up!" Emily called from outside the door.

Andrew heard her try the knob. *Too bad, Em!* he thought. *You can't get in!*

"Andrew?" she called. "I swear, if we miss the late bus, I'll kill you!"

Still smiling, Andrew squeezed a strip of toothpaste onto his toothbrush. He glanced in the mirror.

He froze.

The toothbrush fell out of his hand.

His face! It *was* pale! As pale as milk! No wonder his mother had been worried.

"Andrew!" Emily pounded on the bathroom door with both fists. "Come out of there!"

Andrew didn't bother answering. He kept staring at his face. His skin was the same color as the white tile

18

on the bathroom walls! He peered closer—at his lips. His red lips. His *really* red lips. He saw a smudge of red under his chin. He pulled back the collar of his shirt. Blood! He was bleeding!

Quickly, Andrew tore off a few sheets of toilet paper. He wet them and dabbed at the cut on his neck.

He peered closer. The spot on his neck didn't look like a cut, really. It looked more like a pair of mosquito bites. As if he'd been stuck with a barbecue fork. Or a snake had sunk its teeth into his neck. Or . . . something else had.

A vampire!

Andrew's hand trembled as he felt the two little bumps.

He whisked his hand away.

He stared at the puncture marks.

What did they mean?

Oh, no! Andrew gasped. *Am I a vampire-in-training?*

4

Andrew stared at the mirror—at the holes in his neck—when the bathroom door swung open.

"I did it!" Emily crowed. She held up a twisted bobby pin.

"You . . . you did?" Andrew stammered. He put a hand to his neck. "With *that?*"

"Yes!" Emily cried. "I picked the lock!"

"Oh." Andrew let out a deep breath. "Um, Em? Could you come over here for a second?"

"Sure," Emily said sweetly. She walked over to where Andrew was standing. But before he could ask her to check out his neck, she grabbed his shirt collar.

"Hey! Stop!" Andrew cried. "What are you doing?"

What Emily was doing, he realized, was pulling

him out of the bathroom. She dragged him down the hall.

"I am sick of waiting for you every morning," Emily ranted. "I am sick of having to walk all the way around the pond to catch the late bus!"

"Hey . . . Em?" Andrew began.

"I *hate* being almost late for school every single day!" Emily went on. "I hate going to middle school because *you* go there!"

Andrew tried again. "Emily, stop!"

"I can't wait to go to high school *all by myself,*" she said.

Emily started dragging him down the stairs. Andrew grabbed the banister. Emily pulled. But Andrew held tight.

"Hold it!" he yelled. "I'm ready! I have to get my backpack. That's it. I promise. Thirty seconds. We're out of here."

Emily let go. "Twenty seconds!" she called after him.

Andrew dashed to his room. He grabbed the black book from under his pillow. It still felt cold as ice. How was that possible? As Andrew stuck the book into his backpack, he gasped. The writing on the cover! It was gone! It had disappeared completely.

Oh, man! He had plenty of questions for T.J. He sure hoped T.J. had some answers.

Andrew shoved the icy book into his pack. He

threw on his jacket and ran out of his room. At the bottom of the stairs, his mother handed him a small brown bag. He snagged it with one hand, never slowing his pace. He ran down the sidewalk after Emily.

Mrs. Griffin waved from the front porch. "Have a good day, kids!" she called.

Andrew flopped down beside T.J. on the late bus. He and Emily barely made it. They had to run the whole way.

"What's wrong?" T.J. asked.

Andrew was panting hard, trying to catch his breath.

"What's in the bag?" T.J. asked.

Andrew handed him the bag.

"A hot buttered bagel!" T.J. exclaimed. "Can I have a bite?"

Still panting, Andrew nodded yes.

"Thanks!" T.J. dug in. After a couple of bites, he glanced at Andrew. "You know, you don't look so hot," he said. He leaned closer to Andrew. "What have you got on your face?"

Andrew frowned. He wiped a hand across his cheek.

"It looks like white makeup," T.J. said. He leaned even closer. "And . . . and your lips! Do you have on *lipstick?*"

22

Andrew slumped down in his seat.

"Andrew, what's the story?" T.J. asked. "You look like you're becoming . . ."

Andrew shut his eyes. He waited for T.J. to say the V word.

T.J.'s voice dropped to a whisper. "Andrew, are you turning into a clown?"

Andrew shook his head. He finally caught his breath.

"I am *not* becoming a clown," Andrew said. He glanced darkly at his friend. "But I might be turning into something else."

"What are you talking about?" T.J. asked him. "Um . . . you want the rest of this bagel?"

Andrew shook his head. He stared out the window as the bus crossed Winding Brook Bridge. Then he unzipped his backpack and pulled out the black book. He dropped it on T.J.'s lap.

"Here," he said. "Now tell me how it works."

T.J. popped the last of the bagel into his mouth. He licked his fingers. Then he ran a chubby hand over the blank cover.

"It's so cold," T.J. said. He glanced up at Andrew. "Did you have it in your freezer, or what?"

Andrew frowned. "You mean . . . this isn't your book?"

T.J. shook his head.

"You didn't put it under my bed?"

"I've never seen it before." T.J. handed back the book.

"But if it isn't yours—" Andrew stopped. His heart began to pound. He felt his stomach knotting up. If it wasn't T.J.'s book, then whose was it? Where had it come from?

"It was under your bed?" T.J. asked.

Andrew nodded. "I found it this morning," he said. Then he told T.J. everything. About finding the book. The strange writing. The chapter on vampires-in-training.

When Andrew finished, T.J. shook his head. "Boy, I almost believed you for a minute. You made it sound so real."

"It *is* real, T.J.," Andrew said.

"Come on," T.J. said. "I'm not as easy to fool as Emily."

"There's more," Andrew said. "I went into the bathroom to brush my teeth. I looked in the mirror. I was white as a sheet. My lips looked . . . weird. And then I saw this."

Slowly, Andrew pulled down the collar of his shirt.

T.J. stared at the marks on Andrew's neck. "Nah . . . No way." But he didn't sound so sure anymore.

"Something bit me," Andrew said. "Something with fangs."

T.J. reached out a finger. He ran it over the marks on Andrew's neck. Then he jerked his hand away.

"Oh, wow!" he said over and over. "I can't believe it!"

"Me either." Andrew's voice shook. "T.J., do . . . do you think I'm turning into a vampire?"

5

"**I** wish *I* were a vampire-in-training." T.J. sighed as the bus headed for Park Drive. "Let me look at your bite again."

Andrew glanced around. "Be cool, okay?" he said. "I don't want anybody else asking to see it." He pulled down his collar.

"It looks like the real thing to me," T.J. said at last.

Andrew groaned.

"A vampire bite would explain why you're so pale," T.J. went on. "And the red lips." He grinned. "All you have to do is wait until the tooth marks disappear, and you'll be a real vampire!"

Andrew groaned again.

"You really think a vampire was in your room?" T.J. asked.

"I don't know," Andrew answered. "I . . . I dreamed about a vampire," he said, remembering. "At least I think it was a dream. But . . . maybe not. How else could the book have gotten there?"

"A vampire must have left it for you," T.J. said thoughtfully. "Right after he bit you."

Andrew shuddered at the thought. A vampire in his room! A vampire standing over him in the dark. Bending down. Baring his fangs. Biting him in the neck!

The knot in Andrew's stomach tightened.

"What's wrong?" T.J. asked. "Aren't you excited?"

"No!" Andrew exclaimed. "I'm scared to death."

"Death!" T.J. almost shouted. "That's it! No death!"

"Shhh!" Andrew cautioned him.

"You're becoming one of the undead!" T.J. whispered.

"But I don't want to be undead!" Andrew said. "I want to be alive. Just the way I am right now." He frowned. "I mean, the way I was. Before I got this stupid bite."

"But, Andrew," T.J. said. "Think about it! You're going to be around forever. Forever! And you'll be able to fly. Every night you can go zipping around through the clouds!"

"That part sounds cool," Andrew admitted. "But—"

"You can put people in trances," T.J. interrupted. "You can zap them with your Dracula stare."

Andrew only nodded.

T.J. was on a roll now. "Think about when Emily gets bossy. All you'll have to do is stare at her and . . . bingo! She'll be in a trance! She'll have to obey your every command!"

A small smile appeared on Andrew's redder-than-usual lips.

"Okay, there's some good stuff," he admitted as the bus came to a stop in front of Shadyside Middle School. "But what do I do when I get hungry, T.J.?"

T.J. shrugged. "You'll have to find a victim," he said. "You'll have to . . . go out for a bite!"

Andrew didn't even smile at T.J.'s stupid joke.

"If I turn into a vampire, I'll have to drink blood!" he said. "Think about that! Ugh! It would be horrible, T.J.!"

Andrew followed T.J. down the bus steps with the other students. They headed up the sidewalk.

T.J. stopped in front of the school. "Anyway, you don't have to worry about it," he said. "You're not a vampire."

"I'm not?" Andrew felt a flood of relief.

T.J. shook his head. "You're standing in bright sunlight."

"So?"

"A real vampire can't be in sunlight," T.J. told him. "If sunlight hits a real vampire, it turns him to dust. Too bad."

Andrew watched T.J. run off to his locker. He hoped he *wasn't* turning into a vampire. He hoped T.J. was right. He usually was. After all, T.J. knew everything about vampires.

But, Andrew wondered, *how much does he know about vampires-in-training?*

I could eat a cow, Andrew thought. He stood in the hot-lunch line. He took a plate of spaghetti and meatballs with red sauce. He asked for extra sauce. He wasn't usually crazy about school lunches. But this one looked delicious! He reached for a double side order of bread, a carton of milk, and a huge slice of chocolate cake. Then he walked across the cafeteria and sat down across from T.J.

T.J. eyed Andrew's tray. "What's with all the food?" he asked. "Are you going out for sumo wrestling or something?"

Andrew shrugged. "I'm starved," he said. He didn't waste any more time talking. He dug into that spaghetti. Mmmmm! The sauce was even *better* than it looked! He stuffed a whole meatball into his mouth.

T.J. watched, wide-eyed.

Andrew opened his mouth and gave T.J. a gross-out meatball view. Then he kept right on scarfing down his enormous lunch. The spaghetti and meat-

29

balls quickly vanished. A puddle of red sauce was still on the plate. Andrew tore off a piece of his bread and sopped up the sauce. He popped it into his mouth.

He chewed the bread slowly. It had a funny, sour taste.

Then he grabbed his throat. He made a horrible choking noise.

"Andrew?" T.J. said. "What's wrong?"

Andrew tried to tell him. But he couldn't. The sour taste flooded his mouth. He had to get rid of that taste!

He raked his fingers over his tongue. Oh, no! His tongue felt numb. Totally numb!

And now the tingling feeling swept over his lips.

"Andrew! What's wrong?" T.J. was practically shouting.

But Andrew couldn't answer. His whole face was going numb.

And his throat! He clutched at his throat. It was closing!

His eyes bugged out in horror.

I—I can't swallow! Andrew screamed inside his head. *I can't breathe!*

6

T.J. ran around to Andrew's side of the table. He grabbed Andrew under the arms. He yanked him out of his chair. He spun him around. Then he threw his arms around his middle and began pumping his fist above Andrew's stomach.

"St-st-stop!" Andrew managed at last. "T.J.! Stop!"

T.J. stopped. "Hey, I did the Heimlich maneuver!" he cried.

T.J. waved away the two teachers and the cafeteria monitor who ran over to help. "He's okay now. Everything's fine."

Andrew sank back into his chair, breathing hard.

31

"I know what happened," T.J. said.

"You . . . you do?" Andrew asked.

T.J. nodded. "A meatball got stuck in your throat, right?"

Andrew shook his head. "It was the bread," he said between breaths. "It had poison on it or something."

"Poison?" T.J. said. "On your *bread?*"

"That's what it tasted like," Andrew told him.

"Here." T.J. thrust what was left of his grape juice at Andrew. "Drink this."

Andrew gulped it down. A wonderful coolness filled his mouth. The numb feeling faded. He finished the juice. He took a breath. Then another. The numbness disappeared.

"Oh, man," Andrew exclaimed. "That was scary!"

T.J. stared at Andrew for a few seconds. Then he reached over to Andrew's plate. He took the other half of his bread and tossed it into his mouth.

"T.J.!" Andrew gasped. "Are you crazy? Don't!"

T.J. began chewing.

"Doesn't it taste horrible?" Andrew cried. "Doesn't it make your mouth feel all numb?"

T.J. shook his head. He kept chewing and then swallowed.

"Then . . . it wasn't the bread." Andrew drummed his fingers on the table thoughtfully. "Must have been the tomato sauce."

"No, it was the bread," T.J. told him. "And I was wrong."

"Wrong about what?" Andrew asked.

T.J. leaned forward. "You *are* becoming a vampire," he said.

Andrew frowned. "Why? Are vampires allergic to bread?"

"Not all bread," T.J. told him. "Only *garlic* bread!"

"Garlic." Andrew shuddered. Saying the word almost brought back that horrible sour taste.

"You've read the stories," T.J. went on. "You've seen the movies. Vampires can't stand garlic. And now neither can you."

School seemed to last forever that day. Andrew was glad when it was over. When he got on the bus, he walked down the narrow aisle, past his sister. She pretended not to see him. He walked all the way to the back of the bus and sat down next to T.J.

Right away T.J. started talking about vampires. Andrew tried to listen. But he'd had a hard day. And he'd been up late the night before. Now he could barely keep his eyes open.

"See, ghosts are the living spirits of the dead," T.J. was explaining. "And vampires are the semi-living bodies."

"Uh-huh," Andrew agreed.

"Vampires can do cool things. Like turn into bats or wolves. And they have supernatural strength," T.J. went on. "But ghosts have it easier. They don't have to eat or drink or anything."

But vampires do, Andrew thought. *They have to drink blood!*

Andrew's stomach tightened. He felt sick. He tried to think about something else. Jason. Jason turning into a werewolf. But that only made him think about himself, turning into a—

The bus jolted to a sudden stop. Andrew and T.J. jerked forward in their seats.

"Nice one, Mr. Metz!" someone called out to the driver.

Andrew peered out the window. The bus had stopped right on the entrance to Winding Brook Bridge.

"What's the problem?" someone else called.

"I'm not sure," the driver answered. "The engine's running. But nothing happens when I step on the gas."

Andrew groaned. Things were *not* going right for him today.

"I'll have a look under the hood," Mr. Metz announced.

The driver turned off the engine, climbed out of the bus, and opened the hood. After a few minutes he climbed back onto the bus. The engine started right up. He pressed down on the gas. The bus didn't move.

Everyone groaned. Mr. Metz scratched his head, puzzled.

T.J. gave a sudden gasp. He tugged on Andrew's elbow.

"We have to get off," T.J. whispered.

"What?" Andrew couldn't believe his ears. "Why?"

"Come on!" T.J. insisted. He pulled Andrew out of his seat and to the front of the bus.

"We're walking, Mr. Metz," T.J. said.

"Suit yourself." The driver opened the door of the bus.

Andrew followed T.J. down the steps.

"Hold it!" Emily called. "Getting off!" She hurried off the bus too. "What do you think you're doing?" she growled at her brother. "I swear, Andrew. I'm asking Mom to double my allowance if I have to keep track of you."

"We have to walk the long way," T.J. said as Mr. Metz shut the bus door. "Around the pond. Andrew can't cross the brook."

"Why?" Andrew almost yelled. "What's going on? Why did we have to get off the bus? Why do we have to walk around the pond?"

T.J. only nodded his head in the direction of the bus.

Andrew saw that it was now driving across the bridge.

"It couldn't cross with you on it, Andrew," T.J. said.

"Oh?" Emily whirled around to face T.J. "And why is that?"

"Because," T.J. answered, "Andrew's turning into a vampire."

Emily clenched up her fists and glared at T.J.

"Vampires can't cross running water," T.J. went on. "It's one of the rules. So the bus couldn't go until Andrew got off."

"Oh, come on!" Emily cried. "Do you really think you can get me with another one of your pranks?"

T.J. shook his head. "This isn't a prank. Tell her, Andrew."

Andrew smiled weakly. "I think it's true," he told her.

"Oh, right," Emily scoffed. "My brother, the vampire."

The three of them began walking around the pond.

Andrew didn't feel much like talking. And even after his big lunch, he was hungry. He checked the pockets of his jacket, hoping to find something to eat. He fished out an old chocolate cookie. He started nibbling on it.

T.J. and Emily, meanwhile, kept up a steady argument about whether Andrew was or wasn't turning into a vampire.

When a black Labrador retriever began following them, Andrew didn't think much about it. When that dog was joined by a few more dogs, it didn't seem that odd.

Then one of the dogs started barking.

Andrew turned. He gasped. Behind him stood a pack of dogs!

Now every dog began to bark at the top of its lungs.

"Holy cow!" T.J. exclaimed.

The dogs circled Andrew. He stepped back. "Hey, dogs," he said nervously. "Nice dogs."

He backed away some more. His heart beat hard with fear.

A big yellow dog came around behind him then. It drew back its lips, baring its teeth. A low growl came from its throat.

"Stop!" Emily screamed at the yellow dog. "Beat it!"

The yellow dog only curled its lips in a snarl.

It never took its brown eyes off Andrew.

"T.J.?" Andrew called. He backed up some more. "Help me!"

"Your cookie!" T.J. called. "Maybe that's what they want."

Andrew tossed what was left of his cookie to the yellow dog.

It dropped to the ground. The yellow dog only growled louder, its eyes fixed on Andrew.

"Go home!" Emily yelled over and over. She swung at the dogs with her backpack. But they easily ducked away.

"Get, dogs!" T.J. cried. "Go attack somebody else!"

The dogs circled more closely around Andrew. They drove him back. Away from T.J. and Emily.

"T.J.?" Andrew cried again. "Why are they doing this?"

T.J. yelled something.

37

But the dogs were barking. Barking was all Andrew could hear.

Dogs ran at him from every direction now. They kept coming. Dozens of them, all barking like mad.

Andrew broke out in a sweat. He'd never been so scared.

The dogs barked crazily, their faces twisted with hate.

Their angry eyes glared up at him.

Their white teeth glistened. They snapped at him.

He was beyond scared now. Way beyond. He was numb with fear.

The yellow dog leapt toward Andrew. Reared up on its hind legs, slamming into Andrew's chest. Knocked him to the ground.

Andrew put an arm up to protect his face.

"Help!" he cried as the dogs closed in over him. "Help!"

7

Andrew could hardly breathe. Not with the dogs churning over him. So many of them! Barking and yapping. Drooling and licking him. And the smell. The overpowering odor of dog breath. Andrew squeezed his eyes shut. He was about to be torn limb from limb!

Then the barking stopped. The yellow dog gave a piercing howl. As if it were a signal, the other dogs backed off. They ran in every direction, back where they had come from.

Emily and T.J. rushed over to Andrew. They knelt down beside him.

"Are you okay?" Emily asked.

Andrew nodded from where he lay on the ground.

"Did they bite you?" she asked.

"Of course they didn't," T.J. said knowingly.

Andrew got to his feet. He brushed himself off. "They just sniffed around mostly," he said. "And licked me."

Emily shook her head. "The dogs around here are usually so friendly," she said. "I've never seen them act like that."

T.J. folded his arms across his chest. "This is more proof," he told Emily. "Andrew *is* turning into a vampire."

Emily glared at T.J. "This had nothing to do with vampires!" she shouted. "But something's going on. Something strange." She turned to her brother. "I mean, why did the dogs go after only you, Andrew? Why not me or T.J.?"

Andrew shrugged.

"Because dogs know vampires are their masters," T.J. told her. "Count Dracula called wolves and dogs Children of the Night."

"T.J.!" Emily shouted. "Stop! I mean it. If you say one more word about vampires, I'll . . . I'll . . ."

"Take it easy, Emily," T.J. advised.

Emily sniffed. "Anyway," she said, "it's only three-thirty in the afternoon. It's a little early for Children of the Night."

"Good point." T.J. grinned.

"Can we get going?" Andrew broke in, his voice

40

shaky. "I am not having the greatest day of my life. I'd like to get home."

The three of them headed toward their development. Nobody said much on the way.

When they got to the Griffins' house, Emily went inside. She ran straight up to her room.

"See you, T.J.," Andrew said. He started to go inside.

"Wait," T.J. whispered. "I have to see that book again."

Andrew nodded. T.J. followed him up to his room. Andrew hung up his Do Not Disturb sign. Then he locked the door.

T.J. sat down on the bed while Andrew pulled the book out of his backpack. The black leather cover was blank, the way it had been that morning on the bus. But as Andrew held it, the spidery writing began to show up.

"There!" Andrew exclaimed. "See?"

"What?" T.J. said.

"It's writing the title." Andrew glanced at T.J. "Don't you see it?"

T.J. frowned and shook his head. "I don't see anything."

"You don't? Look." Andrew pointed to the spot where the unseen hand was writing. "Right here."

"Rats!" T.J. exclaimed. "I guess only vampires can see it."

"Vampires-in-training," Andrew groaned.

Andrew sat down next to T.J. He opened the book. The table of contents quickly appeared on the page.

"'Chapter Two,'" he read aloud. "'Vampire Rules.'"

Andrew turned to Chapter Two. Delicate handwriting began to fill the page.

"Is there writing?" T.J. asked.

Andrew nodded.

"So read it!" T.J. said impatiently.

"'As a vampire-in-training,'" Andrew read, "'you must obey the vampire rules. One. Avoid garlic. All parts of the plant will cause you to sicken and retreat.'"

"Now it tells you," T.J. commented.

"'Two,'" Andrew read on. "'You cannot cross running water. You may, however, be transported across a river or stream while sleeping in your coffin.'"

T.J. giggled. "Guess you'll have to ride the school bus in your coffin, Andrew."

"Not funny, T.J.," Andrew said.

"You should have read this part this morning," T.J. added.

"But I couldn't," Andrew told him. "The only writing in the book then was Chapter One. There *wasn't* any Chapter Two."

T.J. rolled his eyes. "Keep going."

"'Three,'" Andrew read. "'You will become appealing to canines. Dogs and their brothers, the wolves, will bark and howl at your approach. They will want to be near you.'"

Andrew slammed the book shut.

"Keep going!" T.J. cried.

"I can't," Andrew told him. "The writing stopped."

"Bummer," T.J. muttered.

Andrew threw the book down in disgust. "This isn't any good!" he exclaimed. "The rules are showing up too late! I've already had garlic poisoning. I've already had a problem crossing running water. And I've already been attacked by a pack of dogs." He shook his head. "If this book is going to do me any good, it has to tell me stuff *before* it happens. Not after."

T.J. looked thoughtful. "Maybe you're ahead of schedule," he suggested. "Maybe you're a super-talented vampire-in-training."

"Yeah, right." Andrew picked the book up again. He flipped to the back. The pages were blank. All blank. Andrew sighed. "I have to know what's coming up," he told T.J. "I have to know the rules! What if I break one by mistake?"

"You might not survive." T.J. frowned. "Look what that garlic did to you."

Andrew groaned. "There has to be a way to make the writing appear," he insisted. "Help me, T.J.!"

T.J. hopped up and turned off the lights. "See anything?"

Andrew shook his head.

T.J. ran to the bathroom. He came back with a glass of water. He sprinkled a few drops on a page.

Andrew squinted hard at the book. "Nothing," he declared.

"I know! Get your mom's iron," T.J. suggested.

When Andrew returned with the iron, T.J. plugged it in. He turned the dial to the lowest setting. "We don't want the book to burst into flames," he said as he ran the iron over a page.

Andrew stared at the book.

Nothing.

"I give up," he moaned. He unplugged the iron, dropped the book, and kicked it back where it had come from—under his bed.

Then he turned to T.J. "Okay, you're the vampire expert. What am I going to do?"

T.J. grew serious. "You have to totally trust me on this, Andrew," he said. "I'll tell you what you have to do. But do you promise to do it?"

Andrew nodded. He was desperate.

"Okay," T.J. said. "The first thing you have to do is get a coffin."

8

"**A**re you crazy?" Andrew cried. "Get a coffin?"

T.J. nodded. "You have to. Vampires sleep in coffins."

"But *why?* I mean, what would happen if I didn't?"

"Vampires can't really rest unless they sleep in a coffin," T.J. said.

"Okay, so I don't get a good night's sleep." Andrew shrugged. "Big deal. I'd rather toss and turn all night in my own bed than sleep in a coffin."

T.J. shook his head. "You might be okay for a few nights. But a vampire has to sleep in a coffin. It's one of the rules."

Andrew sighed. "Yeah, I'll probably read all about it tomorrow in Chapter Three."

"And not an empty coffin either," T.J. added.

"What do you mean?" Andrew asked.

"It has to have some of your native soil in it," T.J. said.

"Native soil?" Andrew's eyebrows arched up. "Soil? Like dirt? Like dirt out of my own backyard?"

"Exactly," T.J. agreed. "Face it, Andrew. Sooner or later you have to get a coffin."

"Oh, great," Andrew groaned. "So how do I get a coffin? Go to Fear Street Cemetery and dig one up?"

"Hey, yeah!" T.J. exclaimed. Then he frowned. "But how would you get rid of the body that's already in it?"

"B-b-body?" Andrew managed to get out. "I don't want a coffin that's had a body in it! If I have to sleep in a coffin, I want a new one!"

"A new one . . ." T.J. repeated. Then he raced for the door.

Andrew threw himself down on his bed. Why was this happening to him? Only this morning he'd been a normal kid. He'd been worried about finding his sneakers. Now he was some kind of a freak. Now he had to worry about finding a coffin!

T.J. rushed back into Andrew's room, flipping through the Yellow Pages. " 'Clowns,' " he said. " 'Coffee. Coins.' " He stopped. "No coffins. Hmmm. I'll try 'Funeral Homes.' Hey, great! They've got ten listings for funeral homes." T.J. picked up the phone.

Andrew couldn't stand to listen to T.J. asking

about a coffin. A coffin for him! He went down to the kitchen. When he came back with a bag of chips, T.J. was frowning.

"What?" said Andrew. "They don't sell coffins?"

"Oh, they sell them." T.J. reached for a chip. "And you can have a not-too-fancy one for only twelve hundred dollars."

Andrew handed T.J. the bag of chips. His appetite was gone.

T.J. thought while he ate. "For tonight," he said, "find a coffin substitute."

"Like what?" Andrew asked.

"A big box. A drawer. A closet." T.J. finished the chips and tossed the empty bag into the wastebasket. "Any small space where you can put your native soil."

That night after dinner, Andrew went out to the backyard and dug up a little native soil. He felt like an idiot. But he didn't want to break any more vampire rules. He put the dirt into a small plastic bag. Then he walked around his house, looking for something that might serve as a coffin.

In the basement, he found a battered cardboard refrigerator box. It was full of old clothes. But it might work.

Andrew pushed the box over on its side. He took out the clothes through one end. He tossed in his bag of native soil. Then he crawled in to try it out.

Andrew lay there with his head at the closed end of

the box. His feet stuck out the other end. The box smelled funny and damp. He didn't think he could handle a whole night of that smell.

"Andrew?" Emily's voice boomed from above the box. "What are you doing in there?"

"Uh . . ." Andrew didn't know what to say. "I'm . . . doing an experiment. For science class."

"An experiment on *what?*" Emily asked. "On how being in a small space affects the human brain?"

"Hey . . . right," Andrew said. "You got it."

Emily bent down. She peered in at her brother. "And have you found that most brains turn to mush?" she asked him. "Or only *your* brain?"

Emily didn't wait for him to answer. She grabbed him by both ankles and yanked him out of the box.

"I don't know why you were in there," Emily said. "And I don't want to know. But it has something to do with vampires. Right?"

Andrew nodded.

"How can you be so stupid?" Emily was practically screaming.

Andrew sat up. He tried to stay calm while he laid out all the evidence for his sister. She'd see. He *was* becoming a vampire. But for every single thing, she had a reasonable answer.

His pale color? A touch of the flu.

The bumps on his neck? Mosquito bites.

The garlic-bread incident? Spoiled butter.

The bus not going over the brook? Simple engine trouble.

The dogs swarming around him? The cookie in his pocket.

Emily went upstairs then. Andrew stuffed the old clothes back into the refrigerator box. He felt a huge sense of relief.

Emily *had* to be right. Vampires weren't real!

With T.J. around, of course he thought he was turning into a vampire. Because T.J. was so into vampires. Because T.J. wanted it to be true! But now, with T.J. gone, he saw that Emily was right. No way was he turning into a vampire!

But . . . what if he was?

Andrew shivered. That was too horrible to think about!

Late that night, Andrew lay staring at the ceiling. The ceiling of his closet.

He hoped with all his might that he wasn't turning into a vampire. But just in case . . . he didn't want to break any more rules. So he made a bed for himself inside his closet.

A closet wasn't exactly like a coffin. But it was shaped like one—a coffin standing on end. And it was dark. Anyway, it was the best he could do on short notice.

Andrew had lined the floor of the closet with

towels. He brought in his pillow. And a blanket. And the bag of dirt.

Andrew didn't like to admit it. But he felt pretty good curled up inside his closet!

Andrew heard something. It half woke him up. He opened his eyes. It was dark. Very dark. For a second, he forgot where he was. Then he remembered. The closet. But why did it feel so different now? Why couldn't he feel the floor?

Andrew had a strange, floating feeling. His head felt heavy.

A muffled voice outside the closet said, "Where is he?"

"His bed hasn't been slept in," came another voice.

Andrew woke all the way up now.

"Where in the world could he be?" a voice said.

Then the closet door swung open. There stood his mom! And Emily! But . . . they were upside down!

Something was wrong.

Horribly wrong!

What was happening to him?

9

Andrew shut his eyes. Then he opened them.

Emily and his mom stared back at him. They had wide-open eyes. And wide-open mouths. But . . . their mouths were *over* their eyes! They were still upside down.

Seeing them like that made Andrew feel sick and dizzy.

"What in the world . . ." his mother's upside-down mouth said.

"Uh . . ." Andrew tilted his head up. He found himself staring at the floor of his closet. Now he realized where he was.

He was hanging by his knees from his clothes rod!

Emily and his mom weren't upside down. He was!

"Get down, Andrew," Emily demanded.

Andrew tried. But he discovered that he couldn't move his arms. They were pinned to his sides by his blanket, which was wrapped tightly around his shoulders. How did this happen? Could he have wrapped himself up like this?

Andrew struggled. Finally he freed his arms from the blanket. He lowered himself to the floor.

"Andrew?" his mom said. "Were you in there the whole night?"

"Yeah," Andrew said slowly. "See . . . it's sort of like . . . practicing for . . . survival training."

His mom's eyes narrowed. "Hanging by your knees in your closet? How is that supposed to help you survive?"

"Well, you know," Andrew said. "In case I was ever in the woods and I had to sleep hanging from a tree branch or—"

"Give me a break!" Emily cut in.

His mom reached out and felt his forehead. "No temperature," she said, tilting her head as she glanced at him. "I thought maybe you had a high fever with hallucinations."

"I'm okay, Mom," Andrew said. "Really." He wished it were true! "I'll get ready for school really fast, okay? Ten minutes."

"You better," Emily growled at him.

His mother shook her head. "All right," she said. "I

52

have to be at work early today. Don't keep your sister waiting."

"No way," Andrew told her. "Don't worry."

He shooed his mom and Emily out of his room.

He shut the door. Then he leaned on it, his mind racing.

This can't be happening! he thought. *But it is! I'm really turning into a vampire!*

Andrew dove for his backpack. He yanked out *How to Be a Vampire*. He flipped madly through its pages. He was becoming a vampire! He *had* to know more about the vampire rules. But . . . no! The pages were blank!

"Please!" Andrew begged the unseen hand. "Write something!"

And as if on command, writing began to appear.

A mature vampire is a day sleeper. At dawn, he retires to his coffin. There, he may sleep with the lid open or closed.

As a vampire-in-training, you still sleep at night. It is best for you to sleep in a coffin. If a coffin cannot be found, any small, dark place will do.

A mature vampire must return to his coffin at daybreak. If this is not possible, a vampire searches for a cave. Or a tree in a dark forest. There, he will hang upside down to sleep, wrapping his wings around his body.

As a vampire-in-training, you must practice sleeping upside down. If possible, wrap yourself in a sheet or blanket before you go to sleep. This will help you get used to having wings.

The writing stopped there.

Andrew started shaking the book.

"Tell me what I need to know *today!*" he yelled. "Tell me things *before* they happen, you stupid book! Not after!"

What if he broke some serious rule? What if Chapter Four said something like: *Any vampire-in-training who says the word "sneaker" will instantly die a horrible death.*

He needed to know what to do. And what *not* to do. He needed to know now! Before it was too late!

"Ten minutes are up!" Emily called from downstairs.

With a groan, Andrew stuffed the book into his backpack. He threw on his clothes and ran down the stairs.

Emily was waiting at the bottom. "Let's go," she said.

"Hold it," Andrew said. "I'm starving."

Emily followed Andrew into the kitchen. "I cannot believe the torture you put me through in the mornings," she told him.

Andrew stuck two pieces of bread into the toaster oven.

"How did you even *think* of hanging upside down in your closet?" Emily continued. "What is wrong with your brain?"

Andrew wasn't listening. He was spreading jam on his toast. Beautiful bright red jam. He sank his teeth into the toast. Mmmm! He couldn't remember anything tasting this delicious, ever!

"We're leaving now!" Emily declared. She grabbed him by his shirt collar. She began dragging him out of the kitchen. Andrew crammed the rest of his toast into his mouth. He barely had time to grab his backpack off the floor.

Outside, Emily let go and marched ahead of him. Andrew shielded his eyes from the sun. He saw lots of kids waiting for the bus. He stopped. He couldn't get on the bus! If he did, it couldn't cross Winding Brook. It would get stuck again.

"Emily!" Andrew shouted. "I'm riding my bike!"

Without waiting for her answer, Andrew turned and ran for the garage. He'd take the long way to school, around the pond. Tossing his backpack into his basket, he hopped on his bike and took off.

Andrew steered down his driveway. He pedaled hard, gathering speed for the hill ahead. He'd never gone this fast before. He shot up the hill, then down. He whizzed along the street. Lampposts and street signs blurred as he passed. He felt the wind against his face as he rode.

"Whooooeeee!" he yelled.

How fast could he go? he wondered. He pedaled harder. He rocketed along the streets of Shadyside, whizzing through intersections, zooming around corners. He wasn't even breathing hard. He wasn't panting. Nothing to it! And then he knew. He had supernatural strength! There was no other way to explain it.

There was no other way he could have gotten to Hawthorne Drive so quickly. He'd almost reached his school. A few teachers' cars were parked in the lot. But not the bus. He'd beaten the bus!

"All right!" Andrew cried. He sped toward the school.

He'd beaten Emily! All her rushing him around, and now he was here first! He couldn't wait until she spotted him! He couldn't wait to see her face!

Andrew hopped off his bike at the curb. He guided it over to the bike rack. He began putting on his bike lock.

"Are you crazy?" someone called.

Andrew glanced up. He saw T.J. running toward him.

"Hey, T.J.!" Andrew said. "Guess what? I beat—"

But T.J. didn't wait to hear. He grabbed Andrew by the elbow. He dragged him inside the front door of the school.

"Are you trying to kill yourself?" T.J. asked. He held Andrew's arm. He dragged him down to the boys' room. He pulled him inside. He shoved Andrew in front of a mirror.

"Look!" T.J. cried.

Andrew kept his eyes glued to the floor. He was afraid to look.

"Look!" T.J. said again. "Look what you've done!"

Slowly Andrew raised his eyes to the mirror.

He gasped!

10

The skin on Andrew's face glowed bright pink. His freckles had turned into blazing red dots. He looked like a total freak!

Andrew put his hands to his cheeks. He thought they'd feel feverish. But his skin was cold. Cold and clammy.

"What's happening to me?" he whispered.

"It's the sunlight, jerk," T.J. said. "Vampires can't be out in it. Remember? Let me check your neck."

Andrew tilted his head. T.J. studied his bite marks.

"Still there," T.J. declared. "So you're not a real vampire yet. Stay here. I'll be right back."

T.J. scurried out of the boys' room. When he came back, he had an armload of clothes.

"I raided the Lost and Found." He dropped everything on the floor except for a navy blue hooded sweatshirt. That he handed to Andrew. "Put this on."

Andrew did.

"What's wrong with you anyway?" T.J. pulled the sweatshirt hood up over Andrew's head. "Yesterday you ate garlic. Today you almost fried yourself." He tightened the cord inside the hood until only a small circle of Andrew's face showed.

"T.J., I have to breathe!" Andrew objected.

T.J. loosened the cord. But not much. "You're almost a vampire," he added as he began tying a bow. "Act like one!"

T.J. stuck a floppy yellow rain hat over the sweatshirt hood. He handed Andrew a pair of white plastic sunglasses. "Sorry," he said. "It was the only pair in the Lost and Found."

Andrew put on the sunglasses. He turned toward the mirror. He looked like a deranged tourist, ready for rain or shine.

"You think Mr. Landis will let me into English class like this?" Andrew asked.

T.J. looked thoughtful. "Talk with an accent," he suggested. "Maybe he'll think you're a new student from some other country."

"From some other *planet*," Andrew said glumly.

"I know!" T.J. said. "Tell him you have sun poisoning. It's a real disease. My uncle Henry used to get it."

"And it's the truth," Andrew pointed out. "Sort of."

T.J. handed him a pair of black wool gloves.

"Every day you're becoming more of a vampire," T.J. warned. "Pretty soon the sun will destroy you." He snapped his fingers. "Instantly! It'll turn you to dust!"

"You mean . . . I can't ever go out in the daytime?" Fear showed in Andrew's face. "I'll never be able to go to the beach? I'll never be able to go swimming?"

"Swimming might be okay," T.J. said. "In an indoor pool."

"T.J.!" Andrew cried. "I don't want to be a vampire! Help me! Please! There has to be a way to turn this thing around!"

T.J. shook his head. "I don't think so," he said. "Anyway, I can't wait until you're a real vampire!"

Andrew drew back from his friend. "Why?" he asked.

"Because then you can make me one!" T.J. explained. "It'll be great! We can hang out together all night and play pranks! We'll scare people out of their minds! And flying! Think about it, Andrew! Flying is going to be so cool!"

Andrew smiled weakly. Okay, if he *was* becoming a vampire, he might as well think about the good parts. He knew who he'd scare out of her mind. Emily! Miss Know-It-All thought *Alien Slime from Mars* was scary. But that was nothing. Not compared to how

60

scared she was going to be when a couple of bats flew in her window!

Andrew thought some more. His smile faded. Scaring Emily was one good thing about becoming a vampire. The only one!

T.J. put up a hand as the first bell rang. "Hey, Andrew! Give me a high five!" he said. Then he added in his best Draculese: "Beink a vampire ees goink to be vunderful!"

That night Andrew lay in his bed. But he couldn't sleep. His mind kept replaying the day. What a horrible day! He'd walked around Shadyside Middle School looking like an idiot. In class kids pointed at him and shrieked with laughter. When he walked down the hall, kids punched their friends and said, "Hey, look! That guy in the goofy sunglasses! That's Andrew Griffin!"

It had been a long, miserable day.

Andrew turned over. Maybe it was his bed. Maybe he couldn't sleep in a bed anymore. But he wasn't ready to go into his closet. Not yet. He was worn out. But he wasn't sleepy.

Andrew threw back his covers. Maybe a snack would help. Milk and cookies. Andrew tiptoed downstairs. He tried to be quiet so he wouldn't wake his mom. She was worried about him. About his red face. About him sleeping in the closet. He didn't want to worry her anymore. At least not yet. Not until he had to break the *big* news. *Hey, Mom? Guess what? I'm a vampire!*

In the front hallway, Andrew shivered. His mom always turned the heat down at night. He began rummaging around in the hall closet, looking for a sweater.

But he found something better than a sweater. Much better! An old cape of his mother's. A long, black cape. Cool!

Andrew carried the cape into the kitchen. The nearly full moon shone in through the big windows. He didn't even need to turn on the light. Andrew put the cape around his shoulders. His mom never wore it anymore. He didn't think she'd mind him trying it on. He fastened the silver clasp.

Wow! The cape seemed to give him a blast of energy! He wished he were outside on his bike. He wanted to ride, to feel that burst of speed again.

Before he realized what he was doing, Andrew began running around the kitchen table. He flapped his arms up and down. He felt light. Lighter than air. Almost as if he were flying. Any second, he might take off!

"Andrew!" Emily's voice boomed into the kitchen.

Andrew caught a glimpse of her, standing in the doorway.

He grinned and pretended not to see her. He kept running and flapping. He circled the table again. Then he leapt at Emily.

"Hey!" she cried, backing away. "Cut it out!"

Andrew veered away from her and circled the table again. Then he lunged over and stopped right in front of her. He stared into her eyes. He felt a rush of energy coming from his own eyes. A power so strong that it startled him. And the strange thing was—he wanted to use it. He wanted to put Emily into a trance!

"Stop!" Emily cried. She glanced away. "I swear, if you ever do this vampire act in front of my friends, I'll murder you!"

Andrew felt himself power-down then. Without her eyes meeting his, the rush of energy left him.

As it did, Andrew started trembling. He realized he was standing in the kitchen. He was wearing his mom's old cape. Over his pajamas! And he had tried to put his sister into a trance! A vampire trance!

He hadn't meant to do any of those things. It was as if *he* were the one in the trance. Not Emily. *He* was the one doing strange things.

A wave of tiredness swept over Andrew then. He brushed by Emily as he walked to the front hallway.

Emily followed him. "Andrew?" she said. "What now?"

He didn't answer. He simply hung up his mom's cape and headed up the stairs.

"Andrew!" Emily called after him. "I've had it with this vampire stuff. I'm not kidding!"

Andrew locked the door to his room. Then he set

63

himself up inside his closet. The same way he had the night before. It wasn't easy, hanging by his knees and trying to wrap himself up in his blanket. But at last he managed it.

He hung there for a long time, thinking.

He started to doze, when he heard a noise.

The door to his room creaked open. Someone was there! In his room!

He heard footsteps. Closer and closer. Andrew held his breath. He felt the pounding of his heart.

His mom had been asleep when he came upstairs. But Emily wasn't, Andrew realized. It was only Emily. She must have picked the lock.

"Beat it, Emily!" he shouted through the closet door.

Emily didn't answer.

"I'm not kidding, Emily!" Andrew yelled. "Go away!"

"I'm not Emily," a low voice answered.

It didn't sound much like Emily.

The closet door swung open.

"Noooo!" Andrew choked on his scream. "Noooo!"

A vampire stood in front of Andrew.

A real vampire!

Andrew still hung upside down. But he could tell the vampire was old. Really old. And sort of hunched over. What hair he had was slicked back on his narrow head. He wore a long, black cape. In the moonlight Andrew saw his pale skin. His red lips. His burning red eyes.

Andrew tried to scream again. But he was too frightened.

"Get down," the vampire said, his voice now high and scratchy.

But Andrew couldn't move. His blood had frozen in his veins.

"Come on, kid!" the vampire urged. "Don't take all night."

Andrew let go. He fell off the hanging rod. Then he scrambled to his feet.

"Step out here," the vampire ordered. "Let me take a look."

Andrew tried to walk to the middle of his room. But he was shaking so much. He didn't know if he could make it.

The vampire circled Andrew, examining him in the moonlight. He put his face close to Andrew's. Andrew saw his red-veined eyes. His dark, stained teeth. Andrew felt his stomach lurch as he breathed in. The vampire smelled like old, spoiled meat.

The vampire stopped circling. "You are so small," he observed. "So puny." He shook his head, clearly disappointed. "I'll have to work overtime to make you worthy of the Dark Gift."

"The what?" Andrew asked.

"The Dark Gift." The vampire gave Andrew a grave look. "The honor of becoming one of us. A vampire."

"I don't want to be a vampire!" Andrew cried. "You better give the gift to somebody else."

"I *never* make mistakes in choosing my victims. Never! Not once in six hundred years!" The vampire sighed. "I have my work cut out for me here. I can see that. But in the end . . ." He smiled. "In the end, kid, you'll be a vampire I can be proud of!"

"But I don't . . ." Andrew began.

The vampire's eyes flashed angrily. "Stand up straight!" he commanded. "No more chitchat."

Andrew straightened up. It wasn't easy. His legs shook under him. His heart thundered in his chest.

The vampire circled him, checking him out.

Dozens more questions popped into Andrew's mind. Did he dare ask them? The vampire said no talking.

Andrew couldn't help himself. "Excuse me, sir?" he said.

"What?" the vampire snapped.

"D-d-did you leave that book under my bed?" Andrew asked. "The one called *How to Be a Vampire?*"

"You figured that out all by yourself?" The vampire rolled his red eyes.

Andrew felt foolish. But he had another question. He put his hand to his neck. "And you bit me too. Right?"

"What are you, a genius?" The vampire shook his head. "Of course I left you the book. Of course I bit you." He raised a fist and knocked on Andrew's head. "Hello? Anybody in there?"

Andrew ducked away from the vampire. "What do I call you?"

The vampire sniffed. "I am Count Ved," he said. "Count Humphrey Ved."

"Humphrey?" Andrew said, surprised.

67

"Why not?" The vampire shrugged. "But you keep on calling me sir. Now, show me your teeth."

Andrew's lips trembled as he drew them back from his teeth.

"What? No fangs?" The vampire shook his head. "You're slow, kid! My last victim grew fangs within hours of my first bite."

"Sorry." Andrew shrugged. "My mom says I was late getting my baby teeth too."

"Baby teeth!" The vampire moaned. He raised his red eyes to the ceiling. "Dark Powers, give me strength!" he muttered. Then he drew a deep breath and glared at Andrew. "First, give me back my book. *How to Be a Vampire.*"

Andrew dug it out of his backpack and handed it to the vampire. "This wasn't any help," Andrew said.

The vampire drew back from Andrew. "What do you mean?"

"The writing always showed up too late," Andrew explained. "After I'd already broken some rule."

The vampire sniffed. "You damaged it, no doubt," he said. He slipped the book under his cape, where it seemed to disappear. Then he reached out a hand with long, yellow fingernails. He grabbed Andrew by the wrist and pulled him over to the open window. "We're out of here," he said.

"What are you doing?" Andrew cried.

"It's time for flying lesson number one," the vampire said.

"Flying?" Andrew tried to yank his arm away.

The vampire held it with an iron grip.

"No!" Andrew yelped. "Don't!"

The vampire pulled him closer to the window.

Andrew glanced down. His bedroom was on the second floor. It was a *long* way to the ground.

The vampire hopped easily to the windowsill. He yanked Andrew up beside him.

"Stop!" Andrew cried. "I can't fly!"

The vampire frowned over at Andrew.

"Never say *can't,* kid," he advised. "Think positive."

Then the vampire leapt out the second-story window.

He pulled Andrew out with him. He let go of his wrist.

"Yaaaaa!" Andrew screamed as he fell.

12

A bright white light flashed before Andrew's eyes.

He screamed again.

The ground came speeding toward him.

He was about to crash! He was about to die!

"Fly!" The vampire's voice sounded inside his head. "Spread your wings."

Andrew didn't have wings. So he spread his arms. Instantly, the ground stopped speeding toward him.

Amazing!

"Now flap!" the vampire's voice boomed. "Flap the wings, kid!"

Andrew pumped his arms up and down as fast as he could. His stomach wobbled, the way it did when he went up in an elevator. Or a plane. Andrew pumped his arms. Up and down. Up and down.

He was flying!

It's a dream, Andrew thought. *A very real dream.*

Andrew peered down. The ground lay below him. He wondered where the vampire was. He turned to the right. He didn't see him. But he saw a wing. A leathery brown wing. *His* wing! He checked his left side. Another wing. Andrew couldn't believe it.

He had wings!

Andrew stared from one wing to the other. He forgot to pump them up and down. He began to tumble through space. He tried to get his arms going again. But he spun out of control. Down, down, toward the ground.

"Idiot!" came the vampire's voice. "Use the wings!"

Andrew stuck his wings straight out. He stopped spinning. The ground settled below him again. He saw the starry sky above. Andrew flapped. He rose. He flapped until he was high above the treetops.

Then he checked himself out. His wings were still there. He peered down at his chest. It looked small and brown and furry.

Yikes! Andrew thought. *I look like a bat!*

"You *are* a bat." The vampire's voice cut into his thoughts. "What did you think you were, a canary?"

I'm a bat? Andrew still couldn't believe it. A bat!

But he still thought like a boy. A boy who could fly.

Andrew felt a rush of wind around him. He glided dizzily on a current of air. He wanted to give himself over to flying. To dive and soar and sail on the air.

But . . . he was terrified! What if he turned back into himself now? Up over the treetops? He'd crash to the ground!

It didn't help to think about crashing. That only made him forget to flap his wings. He tried not to think about what might happen. He thought about now.

Down below he saw a dark ribbon. The river. He wondered how far he'd flown. He wondered if he'd be able to find his way home.

"Follow me," the vampire commanded.

Now Andrew saw something in front of him. It was a large black bat. Of course! The vampire!

Andrew sped through the night, following the vampire. He began to trust his wings. When he tipped them down, they caught air underneath and he rose higher. When he held his wings level, he glided. When he tilted his wings up slightly, they acted like brakes. He slowed down.

T.J. had been right about one thing.

Flying was cool.

"Land at the edge of the woods," the vampire commanded.

Andrew tilted his wings. He followed the big bat as he whizzed lower and lower. Andrew could make out houses now. And street lamps. Telephone wires.

He was coming in fast now.

Too fast!

He couldn't see. Everything blurred. A big brown shape loomed in front of him. A tree. Whoosh! Andrew swerved to keep from hitting it.

Another tree came at him. He almost ran into it. Then he barely missed smashing into the side of a house!

He needed his bat radar. But how did he hook into it? And fast! Before he crash-landed!

Zap! He narrowly missed smashing into a lamp-post!

Bam!

Andrew crashed headfirst into a tree.

A light flashed in front of his eyes.

He fell to the ground.

Andrew lay there, numb.

Then he began to tremble. A pain shot through his wings. His bones groaned and creaked. Then he felt them stretching, getting longer. Growing!

His skin grew tight. And still his bones kept growing, pushing against his skin. Stretching it tighter and tighter until . . .

Andrew heard a hideous tearing sound.

He squeezed his eyes shut.

He knew what was ripping apart.

His skin!

13

The ripping stopped. All at once it was quiet. Very quiet. Andrew heard crickets chirping in the distance.

He opened his eyes. He found himself sitting at the base of a tree. He was barefoot. And in his pajamas. But he had arms. Legs. He had *skin!* Normal, human skin. He shoved up his sleeves and examined his arms. His skin wasn't ripped or torn.

He was his old self again. Andrew Griffin, human.

Andrew bent his arms. He moved his feet in circles. Nothing hurt. His head didn't even hurt where he'd smashed into the tree.

Now Andrew looked around. He was in the Fear Street Woods. But where, he couldn't tell.

"There you are." The vampire towered over Andrew. "Didn't you hear me, kid? I said to land at the edge of the woods."

Andrew shrugged. "I missed." He struggled to his feet. "What were all those awful ripping sounds?"

"Changing you into a bat . . ." The vampire snapped his fingers. "Nothing to it. But changing you back into a boy . . ." The vampire wrinkled his nose as he said *boy*. "That took some doing. But don't worry," the vampire added. "Each time will be easier, kid. The change will be instant when you become a true vampire."

"Um, Mr. Ved, sir?" Andrew said. "Here's the thing. I don't *want* to be a true vampire."

"What did I do to deserve this?" the vampire murmured. Then he glared at Andrew. "What, you didn't like flying?"

"Flying was okay, but—"

"Okay?" Count Ved cut in. "Okay? Do you know how many humans would sell their grandmothers to fly the way you flew tonight?"

"I know." Andrew nodded. "But . . . I'd just as soon take a plane. Really! I don't want to turn into a bat. Or sleep all day. Or . . . or do anything that vampires do."

"Oh, we all start out with these feelings. That's normal. But we learn better." The vampire clapped an arm around Andrew's shoulder. "You'll see. You will develop a *taste* for being a vampire!" He threw back his head and cackled at his own joke.

"I won't." Andrew didn't crack a smile. "Trust me."

"You will!" the vampire insisted. "Trust *me!*" He smiled, showing his awful, rotten teeth.

Andrew shivered. He didn't want to become a creature like Count Humphrey Ved! All decaying and dead-smelling. Never!

"Now . . ." The vampire grew serious. "Very soon your body will reject human food. You'll have to hunt."

"You mean . . ." Andrew began. "You mean I'll have to drink . . ."

"Blood," the vampire finished for him. He rolled his red eyes. "What did you think? Carrot juice? Now, when you hunt—"

"No!" Andrew cut in. "Please! Mr. Ved! Don't make me hunt!"

"But you must," the vampire insisted. "Hunting lesson number one, coming up!"

"Please! Don't make me hunt!" Andrew begged. "Please!"

"You won't start hunting humans, kid," the vampire told him. "You like hamburgers?"

"Hamburgers?" Andrew said. Relief flooded through him. "You mean . . . I'm going to hunt hamburgers?"

The vampire took a deep breath. "No, I'm only pointing out that you eat meat," he said slowly.

"Meat comes from animals. So, you begin by hunting animals. And drinking animal blood."

"No!" Andrew squeezed his eyes shut. He felt sick. He couldn't drink animal blood! He had to find a way out of this!

"Let's get started, kid," the vampire said.

"Hold it," Andrew said.

The vampire glared down at him. "Now what?"

"I can't drink blood," Andrew pointed out. "No fangs."

The vampire's frown changed to a smile. "Hey! Maybe you're not so dumb," he said. "Not `all my pupils think to ask. Okay, here's the thing, kid. Your first prey will be tender. Your own teeth can bite through its skin. You'll drink what blood you can. It's a little messy, but—hey. It's a meal."

Andrew's stomach lurched again. No way could he do this!

"The first thing you have to do . . ." the vampire began.

"I have to go to the bathroom!" Andrew blurted out.

The vampire pointed a finger into the woods. "Then go!"

Andrew took off running. He ran deeper into the Fear Street Woods. He didn't care. As long as he was running away from the vampire. He kept on running. He was getting away! Escaping!

Andrew ran until he couldn't run another step. He stopped in a small clearing. He leaned against a tree, gasping for breath. He had to take off again soon. Before the vampire found him.

Andrew heard leaves rustle. He turned.

He hoped it was a squirrel. Or a rabbit. Or even a bear.

At the edge of the clearing stood the vampire.

But . . . why was he smiling?

"Excellent work, kid!" The vampire rubbed his hands together as he walked toward Andrew. "This is a perfect spot!"

"Spot?" Andrew said, feeling dizzy.

"This clearing." The vampire nodded in approval. "So many burrows. So many tender young bunnies!"

Andrew groaned. Now, how was he going to get out of this?

"Okay, kid, the first thing you need to do is listen," the vampire told him. "Listen for the heartbeat."

"Heartbeat?" Andrew repeated dully. He tried desperately to think up another escape plan.

"The heart?" The vampire leaned toward Andrew. "The thing that pumps blood through the body? The sound it makes is called a heartbeat. Listen for it."

Andrew cocked his head. "I don't hear anything," he said after a few seconds. "I guess I'm no good at hunting."

"Try again," the vampire commanded. "Close your eyes."

78

Andrew closed his eyes. He knew he wouldn't hear a heartbeat. After a while the vampire would give up on him. He'd have to! Andrew pretended to listen.

"Really listen!" The vampire's voice boomed.

Uh-oh. Andrew had no choice. He listened.

He heard wind whistling through the trees. Crickets chirruped in the distance. Wings flapped overhead. Something scampered through fallen leaves. Andrew relaxed. He heard only woodsy sounds. His hearing was still only human. He couldn't hear what real vampires heard. No heartbeat.

Andrew smiled with relief. He opened his eyes.

"Well?" the vampire said. "Did you hear it?"

"Sorry," Andrew said cheerfully. "Didn't hear a thing."

"Concentrate harder," the vampire advised. "I know you can do it. I'm pulling for you, kid."

Andrew closed his eyes again. He thought about heartbeats. How did a heartbeat sound? Lub-dub. Lub-dub. Lub-dub. Lub-dub. At least that's the way it sounded in the film Mr. Kopnick showed in science class last year. Everyone in his class joked around for days afterward, chanting: Lub-dub. Lub-dub. Lub-dub.

Well, there was no way he was going to hear any old lub-dub. He'd just keep his eyes closed a few more seconds. Then he'd open them and say *I can't hear anything*. He'd do it as many times as it took for the vampire to get sick of him and go away!

And then Andrew heard. There was no mistaking it. The sound was nothing like lub-dub. Nothing at all.

It was a small heart. It beat quickly.

Andrew didn't move a muscle. With every part of his body, he listened to the heartbeat. Then, almost without knowing it, he moved toward the sound.

Andrew's mouth began to water.

"Good, good," the vampire whispered softly. "Follow it."

Andrew nodded. He kept his eyes closed. He didn't want to take a chance on losing the heartbeat.

"Follow," the vampire said again. "Go on."

Andrew moved quickly through the woods. He kept his eyes closed. He didn't need to see. His other senses were awake now. Wide awake. He felt a tree before he bumped into it. Somehow he heard the path he was to follow. He kept his focus on the heartbeat. He sensed his prey more strongly with every step.

He came closer. The heart beat more frantically. His victim must sense his coming. But the terrified creature didn't know where to run, where to hide.

At last the heartbeat took over. It filled Andrew's mind. Saliva dripped from his lips. It ran down his chin. He had never been so hungry. He couldn't wait to take his first bite. To taste the warm red blood.

Now! Andrew opened his eyes. In front of him sat a small brown rabbit. It trembled. Its eyes were large and filled with fear. Andrew stared into the frightened eyes. The rabbit didn't move. It was frozen with terror.

Andrew reached out and scooped up the rabbit. He held it close. Its heartbeat filled him with such hunger. He stroked the frightened thing once. But he felt no pity.

All he felt was hunger.

All he saw in front of him was food.

Andrew bared his teeth.

He lowered his mouth to the rabbit's neck.

14

The rabbit's fur tickled Andrew's lips.

He wrinkled up his nose: "Ah-chooo!"

The sneeze drove the heartbeat out of Andrew's head. He wiped his free hand across his nose. He stared at the frightened rabbit in his other hand.

What had he been thinking?

Had he wanted to bite this little bunny? To drink its blood?

No way!

He dropped the rabbit. It darted off into the bushes.

Andrew shuddered. He *had* wanted to drink that rabbit's blood! A wave of sickness came over Andrew.

He'd come so close. That was the scary part. He had *wanted* to drink blood!

Then he saw something even scarier. The vampire! He glided through the trees toward him. What would Count Ved do to him? What was the punishment for letting the rabbit go?

The vampire stopped in front of Andrew. "I have misjudged you," he said.

"I told you," Andrew whimpered. "I don't want—"

"Silence!" The vampire held up a hand. "You talk too much, kid. Way too much. You must listen. Listen and learn."

"Okay," Andrew said weakly.

"Most beginners," he said, "love to feed on animals."

Andrew nodded. He had come close to doing it. Too close!

"They become attached to animal feedings," the vampire went on. "They never develop a taste for human blood."

"You mean . . ." Andrew began. "You're not punishing me?"

"No." The vampire smiled. "I'm happy you let the rabbit go. It is a good sign, kid. A very good sign."

A good sign? Andrew felt shaky as the awful thought hit him: *I'm on my way to drinking human blood!*

"Unfortunately," the vampire went on, "you can't

83

hunt human prey yet. Not without fangs. So that lesson will have to wait."

Andrew heaved a great sigh of relief.

"Your fangs will come, kid." The vampire put an arm around Andrew's shoulder. "Hey, maybe they'll show up in time for *Fangs*giving!" Again the vampire cackled at his own joke.

The two started walking through the Fear Street Woods.

Andrew didn't know which was worse. The vampire's rotten scent—or his rotten sense of humor.

"You're small, kid," the vampire was saying. "But promising. I knew you wouldn't want the rabbit! I felt it in my bones."

They kept walking. The vampire kept talking. But Andrew didn't listen. He thought about that rabbit. He had come so close to drinking its blood! He *never* wanted to come that close again. He had to figure out how to stop turning into a vampire.

Andrew had only one hope: T.J. If anyone could figure out how to stop him from turning into a vampire, T.J. could.

The vampire stopped near Lake Fear. He studied the sky.

Andrew gazed up too. The stars had faded. It wasn't quite so dark anymore.

"Dawn will soon be here," the vampire warned. "Quick, kid! Dig yourself a hole to sleep in."

"A hole?" Andrew couldn't believe his ears.

"Find a stick to dig with," the vampire said. "The earth offers protection. We vampires need to be close to the earth."

"I can't sleep in a hole!" Andrew protested. "I'll smother!"

"Oh, you and your human needs." The vampire gave him a disgusted glance. "I don't have time to argue. Go on home. I'll come for you tomorrow night, kid."

Andrew stared as the vampire's black cape swirled around him. It seemed to swallow him. And then the cape vanished and a large black bat appeared. It flapped its wings, rising ever higher. Andrew watched until the bat disappeared.

Now the sky was filled with pink light. Andrew guessed it was nearly dawn. Good. Nobody would be around. Nobody would see him running home in his pajamas!

Andrew hurried through the woods. The first rays of sunlight stung his skin. He darted for the shade of a large oak tree. From there he ran to another patch of shade. And another. All the long way home Andrew kept to the shadows.

At last he reached his house. He felt under the doormat for the spare key and quietly unlocked the door. He tiptoed up the stairs. His mom and Emily were still asleep. A glance at his clock told him why. It was only six o'clock in the morning!

Andrew checked his face in the bathroom mirror.

He'd turned bright red. His freckles were fried! His skin stung. He put on some of his mom's after-sun lotion. But it didn't help much.

Andrew went back to his bedroom and flopped down on his bed. He felt totally wiped out. What a night!

He lay there. But he couldn't sleep. Andrew rolled over on his back. He didn't have fangs yet. That was a good sign. The vampire wouldn't try to make him drink human blood until his fangs grew in. Maybe they'd never grow in. Maybe he'd never become a real vampire. Maybe.

Anyway, T.J. would know how to undo a vampire bite. He knew everything about vampires. T.J. was his only hope!

Andrew's eyes closed. His thoughts spun inside his head as sleep took him.

He woke with a jolt. Something was wrong. He felt dizzy and sick. His mouth was killing him.

Andrew ran to the bathroom.

He looked in the mirror.

His face was still red.

Then he opened his mouth and screamed.

15

Fangs!

Andrew stared at his mouth in horror.

He was growing fangs!

No. He wasn't growing fangs. He'd already grown them! They sprouted from his gums over his eyeteeth. They were long and white and pointy.

Andrew put a finger to the tip of one. It was needle sharp.

He turned and ran down the hall to his sister's room.

"Emily!" He shook her. "Emily, wake up!"

"It's Saturday, you moron," Emily murmured. "Go away."

"Emily!" Andrew shook harder. "I'm a vampire, Em! A real vampire. You have to help me!"

Emily's voice grew louder with each word as she said, "I am so sick of your vampire jokes, I could scream!"

"This is no joke. I need help," Andrew begged. "Please!"

Emily put her pillow over her head.

But Andrew talked anyway. He told her everything. About the night before. About the old vampire coming to his room. About jumping out the window. About turning into a bat and flying.

Every once in a while he poked the pillow. "Are you listening?" he asked.

Emily nodded.

When he finished, Andrew pulled the pillow off Emily's head.

"It was a nightmare," Emily muttered, her eyes still closed.

"Open your stupid eyes, Emily," Andrew said.

"Promise you'll go away then?" Emily asked.

"Fine," Andrew said. "I'll leave. Just look."

With a sigh, Emily slowly opened her eyes.

"How do you explain these?" Andrew asked. Then he drew his upper lip away from his teeth, showing his vampire fangs.

"Simple." Emily reached out and grabbed the fangs. She tried to pull them out of Andrew's mouth.

Andrew let her try. He wished she could pull his fangs out!

88

At last she stopped. She narrowed her eyes. "Okay, what did you do?" she asked him. "Use Super Glue?"

Andrew shook his head. "They're real, Emily. Real fangs."

Emily climbed out of bed. "Come over to the window, where the light's better," she said. "Let me take another look."

Andrew let her.

At last she stepped back. She put a hand over her mouth. Her eyes were wide.

"Help me, Em!" Andrew pleaded. "What am I going to do?"

"You are disgusting!" she yelled at him.

"What?" Andrew couldn't believe he'd heard her.

"How could you *do* this to me?" Emily cried. "How am I supposed to explain this to my friends?"

"Your friends?" Andrew cried. "Who cares about your stupid friends? What about *me?* I'm the one turning into a vampire!"

Andrew turned and stomped angrily out of his sister's room. What a big help she was! If he did become a vampire, he promised himself to make her life totally miserable!

Andrew dove for his phone and punched in T.J.'s number.

"T.J.?" Andrew said when his friend picked up the phone. "It's happened."

* * *

Andrew headed for the basement. Maybe sunlight wouldn't kill him yet. But he wasn't taking any chances. The basement had only two small windows. He taped black construction paper over them. Then he pulled the chain to turn on the bare bulb that hung from the ceiling. It gave enough light.

A little before eight, Andrew heard T.J. knock. He heard Emily open the front door. Then T.J. came quietly down the basement steps carrying an armload of books.

"I brought my whole collection." T.J. sounded excited. "All my vampire books. I brought them over in my little sister's wagon." He put his books down on the table. "So . . . show me."

Andrew bared his fangs.

"Awesome!" T.J. exclaimed. "Totally awesome! You have to make me your first victim! Promise?"

"Sorry," Andrew said. "But you're here to *un*vampire me, remember? When you do that, I won't be able to bite your neck."

"What a waste," T.J. muttered. Then he dashed upstairs to get the rest of his vampire library.

When he came back, Andrew said, "Being a vampire isn't fun, T.J. It's horrible!"

Andrew told T.J. about the old vampire's visit the night before. T.J.'s eyes grew wider with every detail.

"And last night," Andrew said, "the vampire started teaching me to hunt."

"Cool," T.J. said.

"It isn't!" Andrew yelled. "That's what I keep trying to tell you! I caught this cute little furry bunny. I actually wanted to bite its neck and . . ."

"Drink its blood?" T.J. finished for him.

Andrew only nodded.

"Hmm. I guess vampires-in-training have to sort of work their way up the food chain," T.J. commented.

"But I don't want to!" Andrew almost shouted. "I want to eat pizza and French fries and ice cream. And I want to drink lemonade and milk shakes and soda."

"But what about *tomb*ato juice?" T.J. joked.

"This isn't funny!" Andrew insisted. He sighed. "Come on. Let's hit the books. We have to figure out a way to stop me from turning into a vampire!"

"Andrew?" Emily stood at the bottom of the basement stairs. "I've decided to help you."

"Don't do me any big favors," Andrew said.

"I'm not," Emily said matter-of-factly. "It's for me. You think I want to be known as the girl with the vampire brother?"

"Here." T.J. handed Emily *An Introduction to Vampires.* "This will tell you the basic stuff."

Emily made herself a comfortable seat on some crates. Soon she was twisting her pearl necklace around her finger, the way she always did when she was lost in a book.

T.J. searched through the most advanced books.

Andrew flipped through book after book. He couldn't seem to find anything remotely helpful.

91

Two hours later, they were still at it.

Andrew shook his head. "This book tells lots of ways for a human to turn into a vampire," he said. "But there's nothing about vampires turning back into humans."

He turned to his sister. "Have you found anything?"

"Lots of stuff," Emily said eagerly. "Did you know that if a vampire bites a victim too many times, the victim turns into a werewolf?"

"Emily!" Andrew cried. "This isn't some trivia game! It's a matter of life and death! Stick to vampires!"

"Sorry," Emily muttered. "But this stuff is interesting."

"Only if it's not happening to you," Andrew snapped.

"Right." Emily nodded. "Okay. I read about how vampires hate garlic and mustard seeds. How they hypnotize their victims. How, when they see lots of little things, they can't resist counting them. How they get confused at a crossroads. How they don't reflect in mirrors . . ."

"Hey, I can still see myself in the mirror," Andrew said. "So I'm not a vampire yet. So maybe there's a way to reverse it!"

The three turned back to their books.

At last Emily said, "This book says vampires can't break into a house. They have to be invited in by their victims."

"But only the first time," T.J. put in. "After that they can come and go whenever they want."

"Maybe we can get the vampire who bit you on a technicality," Emily suggested. "Did you invite him in, Andrew?"

Andrew frowned, trying to remember. The vampire had appeared to him the first time in a dream. He knocked on the window. In the dream, Andrew got out of bed and opened the window for him.

"Maybe I did," Andrew said at last. "I thought I was dreaming. But maybe I wasn't."

T.J. slammed a large red book. "There's nothing new in any of these," he said. "There is just the one, classic way to stop you from turning into a vampire."

"What?" Andrew said. "I'll do anything."

T.J. looked into Andrew's eyes. "You have to destroy the vampire who made you a vampire."

"Destroy him?" Andrew's voice squeaked up on the words. "But, T.J.! He's—he's scary! He's a vampire! I'd have to . . ."

Andrew couldn't put the awful thought into words.

"You have to do three things," T.J. told him. "You have to drive a stake through his heart. Then you have to cut off his head. And then you have to stuff his mouth with garlic."

Andrew didn't want to be a vampire.

But he couldn't do any of that horrible stuff!

Or . . . could he?

16

Andrew hung upside down in his closet that night. He didn't know what would happen. But he'd done everything possible to prepare for the night ahead. He was ready. At least that's what he kept telling himself. Over and over and over.

He tried to sleep. He knew he needed his rest. But his mind kept spinning. *What if our plan doesn't work?*

When the old vampire threw open his closet door, Andrew gasped. He'd been expecting it. But he wasn't ready.

Count Ved stood staring at him. His eyes glowed red. His skin was as pale as the full moon.

Without a word, Andrew tossed off his quilt. He

94

hopped down from his clothes rod. He did this with ease now. He was getting used to it.

Andrew glanced at his watch. It was hours until morning. He had to keep careful track of time.

"So, you left your hole." The vampire grinned. "Don't worry, kid. Soon you'll like it underground. Now, open your mouth."

Andrew slowly drew back his upper lip.

"Humph." The vampire shook his head. "Nothing yet."

Nothing? Andrew ran his tongue along his gums. Hey! His fangs were gone! Maybe he was becoming less of a vampire already!

The vampire sensed Andrew's surprise. His eyes narrowed. "Remember the heartbeat?" he asked. "The tender little rabbit?"

Andrew pictured the rabbit. As he did, his fangs slid down.

Oh, no! Andrew thought. *They're back! And he knows it!*

Count Ved broke into a smile. "Congratulations, kid!" he said. "This calls for a change of plans."

"You . . . you mean I have to hunt humans?" Andrew stammered.

The vampire nodded. "The first one is delicious!"

Andrew swallowed. He had to stay calm. He had to stay in control. If he didn't, the plan would never work.

Andrew glanced at his watch again. The plan had

him getting to the Cameron mansion at four-thirty. He had to stall for time.

"I have a question," Andrew said. "Is it true that vampires can change the weather? Can you make it snow?"

"Of course," the vampire told him. "Snow is child's play."

"Let's see you do it," Andrew said. "Right now."

The vampire shrugged. He walked over to the window.

Andrew followed him.

Count Ved seemed only to stare out into the night. But soon Andrew saw small white flakes drifting down from the sky. More flakes tumbled down, thicker and faster. Soon a carpet of white lay on the grass below.

"Cool effect," Andrew told the vampire. "How about a thunderstorm? With lightning and thunder?"

"What, snow isn't enough for you?" The vampire scowled.

Andrew shrugged. "It's okay. If you can't do it . . ."

"Of course I can!" the vampire replied. Again he turned and stared outside.

After a while, the snowflakes grew thick and wet. They turned to raindrops. A strong wind came up. Thunder rumbled in the distance. Andrew saw lightning flash across the sky.

"Wow! We should tune in to the weather channel,"

Andrew told the vampire. "See what they make of all this. I bet it's never snowed at this time of—"

"Quiet!" the vampire ordered. "What's with you tonight, kid? You're babbling like an idiot!"

"Sorry!" Andrew shrugged. "I guess I'm just excited about—you know—being a vampire."

"You are *not* a vampire!" the vampire corrected him sharply. "Not yet. You're still a vampire-in-training."

"You mean there's a chance I won't make it?" Andrew asked, his hope starting to build. "You mean I might flunk vampiring?"

"No," the vampire said. "No one who's started down this path has ever failed. No one has turned back."

"No one?" Andrew's hope dimmed. "Ever?"

"Never," the vampire replied. "See, kid? You'll make it."

Andrew's heart sank.

"Time to go," the vampire said. "Ready to change into a bat?"

"I don't know." Andrew shrugged. "We did bats last night. How about turning us into red mists tonight?"

"I could," the vampire told him.

"And then how about turning us into wolves?" Andrew asked. "Oh, man! I'd love to run around Shadyside as a wolf."

"Wolves and mists. No big deal." The vampire shrugged. "But they're only ways to travel. The main thing is the feeding."

"I know," Andrew said. "But it's not even two o'clock yet. We have the whole night to . . . feed. Come on. Make me a mist!"

"All right, kid. All right," the vampire said. "But only a small one. Mists are tricky."

For a minute, Andrew didn't feel anything. And then he began to shake. He teeth chattered. His fingers trembled. But he didn't feel cold. He felt warmer and warmer. Then hot. A red-hot mist!

Andrew couldn't see exactly. But he felt everything. He was everywhere in his room at once. He pulled himself together and drifted toward the window.

"Oh, no, you don't!" the vampire's voice warned him. "Stay in here. I don't want you getting blown to the south pole!"

Andrew drifted away from the window. He floated slowly out the door of his room and down the hallway. The door to Emily's room was shut. But so what? Andrew the mist slid easily through the tiny space between the door and the door frame. Nothing to it! He filled Emily's room and then slipped back out the way he had come in.

The vampire waited for him at the doorway to his own room.

Andrew slid past him. He hovered over his bed.

98

Before he realized what had happened, he was sitting on his bed, shivering.

"That was totally awesome," Andrew told the vampire.

"Right," the vampire agreed. "And useful, too, if anyone slams the door in your face."

"How about changing me into a wolf?" Andrew asked.

"Not now," the vampire told him. "I have to get started with your lesson, kid. Tonight you're going to track your first human prey. Humans are trickier than rabbits." The vampire leaned closer to Andrew. "But much tastier. They're worth the trouble."

The village clock chimed three as the vampire began hunting lesson number two. He explained how to listen for a human heartbeat. How to follow it. How to hypnotize a victim. How to find the juicy artery that runs along the side of the neck.

"Now," the vampire said when he had finished, "have you got all that, kid?"

"I'm not sure," Andrew said. "Could you go over the stalking part again?"

The vampire sighed. Then he repeated the stalking instructions. *"Now* have you got it?" the vampire asked him.

Andrew nodded. "I think so."

He needed to stall only a little more.

"And I know who I want for my first victim,"

Andrew went on. "See, there's this kid who gives me a hard time in art class. Once he pushed my face down in a bunch of wet plaster, and he held me down for so long, I practically smothered. Finally our art teacher came over and pulled my head out, and—"

"Stop!" the vampire cried. "I don't care about your puny human activities! We have to get on with our hunt!"

"Right," Andrew agreed. "Anyway, I know where to find this boy. Some kids dared him to spend the night at the Cameron mansion."

"That old abandoned house?" the vampire asked. "The one next to the cemetery?"

"That's the place," Andrew said.

"That's where we'll go," the vampire said. "I'm impressed with your eagerness, kid," he added. "Some of my pupils don't want to hunt their own kind. Not for a long time. Let's go."

"Wait," Andrew said. "I better go to the bathroom first."

"No!" The vampire clamped his hand on Andrew's wrist. "Enough of your delays. We're going now!"

17

Andrew felt himself shrinking.

He blinked.

Lights swirled around him.

Everything was out of focus.

He felt himself leaping through space. Then he hit the ground running. He ran faster than he ever imagined he could.

He sniffed the air. The smells! So many of them. And all so exciting! He lifted his chin and gave a great, long howl.

"Quiet, you fool!" came the vampire's voice inside his head. "Do you want the dogcatcher coming after us?"

Andrew turned his head. Racing along beside him was a large gray wolf. A wolf with fiery red eyes.

That's when Andrew knew that he, too, was a wolf.

They ran past the hospital, keeping to the shadows. Andrew sensed small animals fleeing in their path.

Now the Fear Street Cemetery came into view. And the Cameron mansion. Andrew slowed his pace.

"Hey!" the vampire called. "Keep running!"

"Let's check out the woods!" Andrew yelped. "Come on!"

Andrew took off. He cut through yards and sped across Fear Street. He dashed into the woods.

The vampire caught up with him.

"Stop this!" he demanded. "We must hunt!"

"I know," Andrew told him. "But I'm not ready to stalk my victim yet. I want to wolf around for a while."

The vampire wolf drew his lips back, baring his long, white teeth. He gave a horrible snarl.

"I see your point," Andrew said. "Enough wolfing around. Let's get on with the hunt."

Andrew trailed the vampire back toward the village. They stopped in a grove of trees outside the mansion. Andrew regained his human form without much ripping or tearing.

"The boy you're looking for," the vampire whispered. "Is he inside the mansion?"

Andrew nodded. "He's spending the night . . . no, wait!" Andrew pointed to a winding pathway that led from the cemetery to the mansion. "There he is! He's walking toward the house! See him? In the big, bulky coat?"

"A brave lad," the vampire said. "Or an incredibly stupid one—to be walking in the cemetery at this time of night. Can you sense his heartbeat?"

"Loud and clear," Andrew answered. "Oh, man! This kid is going to be so sorry he ever picked on me!"

"Excellent!" the vampire exclaimed. "Revenge and food—perfect together!" He smiled down at Andrew. His fangs gleamed in the moonlight. "I knew you had the right stuff, kid. Go on. Go get him. Remember everything I taught you."

Andrew nodded. He held his breath and listened.

There it was. A heart beating. But this was no small rabbit heart. This was a human heart. Pumping human blood with every beat.

Andrew crouched down. He began moving toward his victim. He moved silently, speedily.

His fangs slid down. Saliva began to drip from them.

Inside Andrew's head the beating of the heart grew louder.

It sounded like a drum, beating and beating.

Andrew drew closer.

He raised his arms.

He bent his knees and sprang at his first victim.

18

〰️

"**H**ey!" cried the boy. "Let go! Help!"

Andrew grabbed him around the neck.

"Don't!" the boy wailed. "Stop!"

Andrew wrestled him to the ground. He put a hand over his mouth.

"Ummmmph!" the boy cried. He kept struggling.

Andrew muffled a laugh.

T.J. was really into his acting job!

Andrew picked T.J. up by the collar of his big coat. He pretended to slam his head on the pavement.

T.J. pretended to be knocked out.

Andrew dragged his victim up the rickety stairs of the Cameron mansion. He pulled him inside the deserted house.

At a distance, the vampire followed them inside.

Andrew pulled T.J. into the living room. It was filled with old, dusty furniture. A big, overstuffed couch. And tattered, overstuffed chairs.

Andrew grabbed T.J. under his arms and lifted him up. He shoved him into one of the chairs.

T.J.'s head rolled on his neck. He groaned. Then he blinked his eyes open and looked around.

"What . . . ? What's going on?" T.J. said. He tried to get to his feet.

Andrew pushed him back into the chair. "Quiet!" he snapped.

Then Andrew turned to the vampire. "Now what?" he whispered.

"Think about what I told you," the vampire coached him. "The artery, kid. Go for the artery."

"Oh, right." Andrew examined T.J.'s neck.

T.J. moaned and rolled his head around some more.

Andrew turned back to the vampire. He shrugged. "I—I can't see it," he said.

The vampire strode over to T.J. He pressed a long, yellow fingernail to T.J.'s neck.

"There," he said. "That's the artery. It's pulsing plainly."

T.J. stared at the vampire. His eyes were wide. His mouth hung open slightly. He started to tremble.

The vampire stared coldly back at him.

Then a strange look came into T.J.'s eyes.

Andrew gazed down at T.J.'s neck. The artery pulsed invitingly. Andrew drew his lips back.

"Stop!" T.J. screamed. "Get away!"

Andrew barely heard T.J.'s scream. All he heard was his heartbeat.

T.J. bolted out of the chair. He shoved Andrew away. He ran for the door.

Andrew tackled him in the hallway. He dragged T.J. back into the living room and pushed him into the chair.

"Good, good," the vampire said. "Now go for his neck."

Andrew leaned over T.J. He felt his fangs begin to tingle.

"Andrew?" T.J. whispered weakly.

Andrew blinked. At the sound of his name, his fangs stopped tingling. Saliva stopped dripping. He straightened up, glancing away from T.J.'s neck. He moved his thoughts away from the blood throbbing through T.J.'s blood vessels. He tried his hardest not to sink his teeth into his best friend's neck!

He had to think of something else—and fast. He pictured his room. The Super Bowl poster over his bed. The Archie comics on his bedside table. His guppies swimming around in his fish tank.

It worked.

His fangs slipped back up into his gums.

Andrew let out a sigh of relief. The plan was going

to work! It had taken a long time for T.J. and Emily to convince him that he could do it. But now he felt sure. The plan was going to work!

Andrew leaned over T.J. He pretended to examine his neck as he whispered in his ear, "Okay, T.J. Hand me the stake."

19

"**T**he stake, T.J.!" Andrew whispered again.

T.J. stared straight ahead. He didn't move.

"Give it to me!" Andrew mouthed the words. "Now!"

T.J. only sat there, still as a statue. Frozen!

Andrew's own heart began to pound. Why didn't T.J. open his coat? Why didn't he hand him the stake the way they'd planned?

Andrew straightened up. He turned toward the vampire.

"Uh . . . why isn't he trying to get away?" Andrew asked.

The vampire smiled at Andrew. "I hypnotized him

for you, kid," he explained. "Since he is your first victim, and all. He's ready for you."

Andrew stared back at T.J. This hadn't been part of the plan! Now what? Maybe he could reach into T.J.'s coat and grab the stake. But T.J.'s coat was buttoned up. It would take too long. The vampire would know something was fishy.

"Well?" the vampire said. "What are you waiting for?"

"I don't want to rush it," Andrew said. He felt trapped.

Andrew stared at T.J. At his neck. He saw the throbbing artery. His fangs slid down again. They began to tingle.

Andrew swallowed. T.J. always said he wanted Andrew to bite him. He wanted Andrew to promise to make him his first victim. Well, Andrew was about to keep his promise.

Andrew stopped thinking human thoughts. He gave in to the tingling feeling in his fangs. He concentrated on the artery. On the blood flowing inside it. Andrew bent over T.J. He drew close to his neck and opened his mouth.

"Andrew! Stop!" Emily raced out from behind the big, overstuffed sofa. She waved a wooden stake in the air.

Andrew straightened up. Emily! What was she doing here?

The vampire whirled around, snarling at Emily.

Emily screamed. She ducked back behind the couch.

Then it all came rushing back to Andrew. The plan. The stakes. T.J. and Emily were there to help him destroy the vampire!

Andrew shook his head. He cleared his mind of his vampire thoughts. His fangs slid back up into his gums.

The vampire seemed stunned by Emily's appearance.

Andrew went into action. He grabbed T.J. and pulled him to his feet. "Wake up, T.J.!" he cried. "Quick!"

T.J.'s head rolled around on his neck for real. Two wooden stakes fell out from the bottom of his coat.

The vampire streaked across the room to Andrew.

Andrew let go of T.J. He slumped back into the chair.

Andrew turned to see the vampire lunging at him. Red sparks flew from his hate-filled eyes.

"You!" He stabbed a bony finger at Andrew's chest. "You planned this! You thought you could defeat me! Ungrateful human!"

"No!" Andrew cried. "I—I didn't do anything!"

The vampire folded his arms over his chest.

"I have lived six centuries!" he cried, his eyes flashing red anger. "You think you can fool me this easily?"

"Me?" Andrew tried to sound innocent. His mind spun. He tried to think of what he should do. "I'm not trying to fool you!"

The vampire scowled and shook his head. "To think I was going to give *you* the Dark Gift!"

"You mean . . . you're not going to?" Andrew asked.

"That's exactly what I mean, kid," the vampire said.

Andrew let out a long sigh of relief.

"You're not getting the Dark Gift now," the vampire said. "You're getting death." He smiled. "I'm going to kill you."

20

"**K**ill me?" Andrew cried. "No!"

"Yes," the vampire said. "All of you."

Andrew heard a noise behind him. He turned.

Emily was making a break for the door!

Go, Em! Andrew thought. *Get away! Bring back help!*

But the vampire was too fast for her. He pounced for the door. He reached out. His hand caught Emily's necklace.

Emily made a choking sound.

The vampire pulled on her necklace. He brought her slowly back into the room. He smiled. His fangs gleamed sharp and white. He glanced from Emily to T.J. and back to Andrew.

"Three juicy humans," he said. "Looks like it's my night for a three-course dinner."

"Kill me," Andrew volunteered. "But let them go."

"Not a chance." The vampire rubbed his withered hands together. Then he reached out and grabbed Emily's necklace again. "I think," he said, "I'll begin with *you,* sweetie."

He tugged on Emily's pearls.

Emily shut her eyes as the vampire pulled her nearer.

Andrew wished he could do something. But what? He was only a vampire-in-training. He was powerless against a real vampire.

The vampire pulled Emily close.

Andrew saw Emily wrinkle her nose as she breathed in the vampire's foul stench.

"Gross!" Emily cried. She pulled suddenly away.

Andrew heard a small *pop* as Emily's necklace snapped. Dozens of pearls clattered to the floor.

The vampire froze. He stood staring at the floor—at the string that had held the pearls in his hand.

Andrew glanced down. Pearls were everywhere! Rolling under chairs. Under the sofa. How many of them? Two, four, six . . . So many beautiful pearls!

Emily grabbed Andrew's arm. "It's true!" she whispered. "Look! He can't resist counting little things!"

"Huh?" Andrew blinked up at Emily. He saw the vampire counting her pearls. He, too, stared back down at them. Where was he? Ten, twelve, fourteen . . .

"Forget the pearls!" Emily tugged on Andrew's shirt. "Come on!"

Emily dragged her brother over to T.J. The sight of his friend staring straight ahead brought it all back to Andrew.

"Help me pick him up, Andrew," Emily insisted. "We have to get out of here!"

Andrew and Emily each grabbed one of T.J.'s arms. Together they dragged him out of the living room and into the hall.

They stopped at the front door.

"We can't drag him all the way home," Andrew pointed out.

Emily nodded. "We have to get him out of his trance."

"T.J.!" Andrew shook him gently.

"Wake up!" Emily snapped her fingers in front of his face.

T.J.'s eyes still gazed at nothing.

"T.J.!" Andrew shook him harder. "Come on! Wake up!"

T.J.'s body stayed limp.

Emily drew back a hand and smacked T.J.'s face.

"Ow!" T.J. cried. He put a hand to his cheek. "That hurt!"

"Sorry," Emily whispered. "Hurry, Andrew. Open the door!"

Andrew turned the knob. He pulled on it. It didn't budge.

114

Emily tried to open it too. She jiggled the locks and twisted the knob with no luck.

"The vampire must have locked it," Andrew said.

T.J. fiddled with the locks and bolts. Nothing worked.

"Come on!" Emily said. "We'll go out the back door."

"Wait!" Andrew cried. "We'll have to go by the vampire. What if he's finished counting?"

"We'll have to take our chances," Emily said. "It's the only way out."

The three ran toward the other end of the mansion.

Andrew zoomed straight for the kitchen door. He turned the knob. Nothing happened. The back door was stuck. Andrew tried to fling open one of the kitchen windows. No use. It was nailed shut.

"He'll be finished counting any minute!" Andrew wailed.

"Listen!" Emily's eyes grew wide. "I hear footsteps!"

Andrew heard them too. His sister was right. The vampire was coming!

Andrew's eyes darted around the room, searching for a way out. The windows were shut tight. The door was stuck. The only other door led to the hallway.

But that's where they heard footsteps!

That's where the vampire was about to appear!

"He's got us!" Andrew cried. "We're trapped!"

21

~~~

The footsteps sounded louder. They came closer. Closer to the kitchen. The old floorboards creaked and groaned.

Andrew, Emily, and T.J. huddled together. They pressed against the far kitchen wall.

"What time is it?" Andrew whispered.

"Funny you should ask, kid!" the vampire's voice boomed as he stepped into the room. "It's time for you to die!"

Andrew squeezed his eyes shut. No way was he going to let the vampire hypnotize him. Emily and T.J. pressed closer to him. He felt them trembling.

Then Andrew felt them stop trembling. Their bodies relaxed. Andrew opened his eyes. He glanced at T.J. He stared straight ahead. Oh, no! The vampire had put him into another trance!

Andrew turned to Emily. She stared straight ahead. Just like T.J. The vampire had hypnotized both of them!

T.J. slumped to the floor. Emily dropped beside him.

Now it was only Andrew—and the vampire.

The vampire smiled, showing his long, white teeth. "Eenie, meenie, miney!" he counted, ending with Andrew. "You die first!"

Without thinking, Andrew put up his hands to cover his neck.

"No, no, no." The vampire stepped toward Andrew. "I've decided not to bite you." He gripped Andrew's shirt with his fist. "I won't take a chance on giving you the Dark Gift. You're not going to be undead, kid! You're going to be dead dead!"

Andrew tried to back away.

"I made a mistake choosing you," the vampire growled. "A bad mistake. But then, it's the first mistake I've made in six hundred years. That's not too bad. Still, it was a mistake."

Andrew nodded. He agreed. A big mistake. There was no way he could run now. No escape. The vampire was too fast. Too strong.

I'm history, Andrew thought.

Right then he wished he'd been a better vampire-in-training. Even biting bunny necks seemed better

117

than being dead forever. But Andrew really wanted to be what he was right this minute. *Alive!* Andrew had to do something to keep it this way. He had to try!

Andrew jerked suddenly to the right. He took the vampire by surprise. The fiend lost his grip. Andrew didn't waste a second. He leapt over T.J. and sprinted across the room.

"You know what, *sir?*" he shouted. "It's too late!"

The vampire snarled horribly. His eyes shot hot red sparks.

"Too late for what, kid?" he asked.

"Too late to take back the Dark Gift," Andrew cried. "I've already got it! You're too late to stop it!"

Andrew kept his eyes away from the vampire's. He drew his lips back from his teeth. His fangs slid down. He bared them and snarled at the vampire. "And one more thing!" he shouted. "Humphrey is a stupid name for a vampire!"

With a growl, Humphrey the vampire lunged across the room.

Andrew darted away.

He glanced toward the little window in the kitchen door—and another plan sprang to his mind. Only before he could dodge away, the vampire was on him.

He shoved Andrew against the kitchen door.

Andrew's nostrils filled with the foul reek of the undead.

He felt the vampire's hands close around his neck.

Cold fingers gripped Andrew's throat, choking him.

Andrew struggled for breath. He thought of his plan. It gave him strength. With all his might he pushed the vampire away.

The fiend staggered back. But he recovered quickly.

He dove for Andrew. Andrew leapt out of the way. He darted to the far side of the kitchen.

"Come and get me, Humphrey!" he cried.

With a terrible snarl, the vampire bared his fangs. He raised his hands and charged at Andrew.

Andrew arched his back, dodging away. He smelled the vampire's foul breath. Felt his bony fingers scrape against his neck. But he escaped.

Andrew leaned against the kitchen door. His heart pounded. He tried to stay calm as he reached behind his back. Slowly he turned the doorknob.

"You'll never get me!" Andrew shouted. "Never!"

The vampire let out a growl as he bent his knees. Then he sprang off the floor. He flew across the room at Andrew.

Andrew pulled as hard as he could at the doorknob. The kitchen door flew wide open. He jumped aside.

The vampire shot out the door.

Andrew slammed the door behind him. He knew he had to keep the vampire out! Andrew leaned all his weight against the door. He stared out its little window. If this didn't work, he was dead!

Count Ved whirled around. He lunged at the door, screaming.

22

~≈~

Andrew drew back from the door.

But the vampire stopped short. For a moment, he froze in place. The fiend reached up and grasped his own white neck. He stared up at the sky and realized—he was standing in a patch of sunlight!

The vampire shuddered. A thin wisp of smoke rose from the top of his head. A terrible scream escaped from his throat. Then his whole body vanished in a cloud of smoke.

Gone!

Andrew smiled. *Sunlight.* Why hadn't he thought of that in the first place? It was much easier than staking the vampire. Much less messy too. And best of all—it worked.

Andrew opened the door and stepped outside. All that remained of the vampire was his cloak. It lay on the ground under a small pile of dust.

Andrew's mind tried to grasp what had happened. He didn't die. And he wasn't going to!

It was the vampire who was dead. Dead and gone forever!

As Andrew caught his breath, he spotted something on top of the pile of dust. He bent down for a closer look—and saw what it was. Two gleaming white fangs.

Andrew reached down and picked them up. The pointy teeth weighed nothing. He slipped them into his pocket.

Andrew stumbled back into the Cameron mansion.

T.J. and Emily were still on the floor. But with the vampire destroyed, they were coming out of their trances.

T.J.'s eyes grew wide when he saw Andrew. "You're alive!"

"Looks that way," Andrew said.

"But where's the vampire?" T.J. asked, gazing around.

"Outside," Andrew answered. "Getting a little sun."

"You mean . . ." T.J. began. He broke into a grin.

Andrew nodded. "We got him, T.J.," he said. "He's history."

"What about you, Andrew?" Emily asked, getting

to her feet. "Are you unvampired? Let me see your neck."

Andrew pulled down the collar of his shirt. He waited while Emily examined his throat.

"The tooth marks are gone," Emily told him. "You're okay!"

Andrew smiled. "Come see what's left of the vampire," he said. He led the way out the kitchen door.

There they saw the black cape. And the little mound of dust.

"Let's get out of here," Emily said.

"Really," T.J. agreed. "I want to hit the sack and sleep for about two weeks."

T.J., Emily, and Andrew followed the path away from the Cameron mansion. They headed for their development.

At the footbridge over the river, they stopped.

"Well, this is the test," T.J. reminded Andrew. "If you can cross it, then you're definitely not a vampire."

"And if I can't?" Andrew asked.

"Then I guess you'll be out hunting tonight." T.J. giggled.

Andrew thought for a moment. "You know," he said at last, "I think I'll take the long way home. For old time's sake."

"Andrew!" Emily said impatiently. "Don't be silly. We have to get home. You're going over the bridge. Stop fooling around."

"I'm not fooling around," Andrew said calmly. "I just feel like walking the long way."

Emily folded her arms across her chest. "I absolutely forbid you to go that way. Now, move it, android. Over the bridge."

Andrew said, "Emily? Are you getting . . . bossy?"

"So what if I am?" Emily retorted. "It makes no sense to take the long way home. After the night we've had. I can't believe you even want—"

"Emily?" Andrew interrupted. "Be quiet."

Then he smiled at her, drawing his lips back from his teeth. Two long white fangs glinted at her in the early morning light.

Emily's eyes grew wide with terror. She put a hand to her mouth and then ran over the footbridge, screaming.

Andrew and T.J. watched her go.

"Hey, Andrew," T.J. said. "I'm confused. Are you a vampire or not?"

Andrew put his hands to his mouth. He pulled two white fangs off his own eyeteeth. He held them in the palm of his hand.

"They're Count Ved's," he told T.J. "It's all that was left of him." He grinned. "Poor Emily," he said. "You'd think she'd be used to our pranks by now."

"Yeah," T.J. agreed. "But she falls for them every time."

Andrew slipped the fangs back into his pocket.

123

"Walk the long way home with me, T.J.," he said. "Okay?"

"Sure," said T.J. They began walking. "So . . . I'm not clear on exactly what happened. You must have staked the vampire right before the sun hit him. Right?"

Andrew shook his head. "I didn't stake him," he said. "Lucky for me the old guy didn't know about sunscreen."

T.J. frowned. "But, remember what my book said? Sunlight kills a vampire. But that's all it does. It doesn't remove the curse from the vampire's victims. Only *staking* can do that."

"Huh?" Andrew said. He was only half paying attention to T.J.

"Absolutely," T.J. told him. "I mean, you can't exactly drive a stake through a pile of dust, so I guess it's too late. What do you think, Andrew?"

Andrew glanced at T.J.'s neck. He saw his artery there.

"Andrew?" T.J. said. "I asked if you think it's too late?"

"Oh, yeah," Andrew replied. "I think so."

"Andrew?" T.J. said again. "Why are you looking at me like that?"

Andrew's fangs slid down now. He turned, smiling at T.J.

"Very funny, Andrew," T.J. said. "But you already did that trick."

Andrew reached into his pocket. He put his hand around the vampire's fangs and pulled them out. He showed them to T.J.

T.J. glanced at the fangs in Andrew's hand. Then up at the fangs that were part of Andrew's smile.

"Wait," T.J. said. "Hold it. You can't be a vampire. You're out in the sun. Unless . . . you mean . . . does sunscreen really work?"

"Uh-huh." Andrew felt his fangs tingling now.

"Whoa! You really are a vampire!" T.J. exclaimed. "That is so cool, Andrew! You have to tell me what it's like. I'm *so jealous!*"

Andrew moved closer to T.J. Gazing at his neck. Soon, Andrew would not have to tell T.J. what it was like to be a vampire. T.J. would not have to be jealous anymore. Very, very soon, T.J. would understand everything.